THE
NIGHTMARE ROOM

CHRIS SORENSEN

Harmful Monkey Press / Sparta, NJ

For Debbie

CHAPTER 1

The boy woke to the sound of his own screams. He quickly extinguished his cries, hands clasped over his mouth. Had he caught himself in time?

No…

He heard the creak of a door opening down the hall. The Old Man was awake.

"Goddamn it, boy!" his father roared. *"Goddamn it!"*

The man staggered into the doorway, his hair a tangle. He was wearing a stained flannel shirt and grey work pants held cinched about his thin, knotted frame by a thick belt three notches too big. His grizzled face was a mix of anger and annoyance.

"I'm sorry," the boy squeaked, trying to pull the wool blanket up over his nose.

"Do you know what time I have to get up? I need my damn sleep!"

"I'm sorry!"

"Sorry don't cut it!"

As the man stepped into the room, the boy's bladder let loose a warm stream, soaking his PJs and the sheets.

The man yanked off the covers and recoiled. "Jesus! Did you piss yourself? Je-sus!"

"I'm sorr—"

His father smacked him hard across the face with the back of his hand. The boy's cheek went red.

"Get up. Get up, get up, get up!" the Old Man shouted. "Are you deaf? Get up!"

The boy did as he was told. He was soon standing before his father, the legs of his rocket ship PJs—a prized find at the local Goodwill—soaked in urine.

His father looked down at him in disgust. "Six and still wetting the bed like a baby."

"Seven."

"What'd you say?"

The boy tensed. He knew he risked another slap, but for some reason he couldn't help himself. "I'm seven. Not six."

The Old Man bared his teeth, but the blow never came. Instead, his father grabbed him by his collar and dragged him from the room—like a dog from its cage.

Unable to keep up, the boy's feet slid across the buckled and sagging hardwood floor. More than once the odd splinter stabbed his soles, causing him to wince but not to cry out. Never to cry out.

His father grabbed the banister and proceeded down the stairs, his son thumping along behind him. The boy squirmed to avoid the constant cracking of his ankles against the steps below.

"Should know better than to let you sleep in your bedroom," the Old Man grumbled as he reached the foot of the stairs. His thought was interrupted by a wide-mouthed yawn that caused his jaw to crack. "God, I'm dead tired."

As the boy continued to stumble after his father, he found himself taking mental snapshots of the rooms they passed. The dining room, once complete with dining table, now a storeroom for the boxes of 'treasures' the Old Man swiped from his garbage runs. *Snap!* The kitchen containing the useless stove and the microwave oven the size of a Buick. *Snap!* The hall closet still filled with his mother's coats, jackets and hats. *Snap!*

The boy pinwheeled as his father rounded the corner; he heard the neckband of his PJs rip. The basement door was coming up fast, and a sour, sinking feeling curdled the boy's gut.

"I'll be good. I'll be quiet," the boy pleaded.

"Tell it to the Marines," the Old Man snarled.

The man threw open the basement door. A rush of mildewed air rose up from the darkness, like the hideous breath of some subterranean *thing*. He flicked on the light, and the cascade of descending stairs came into view. Among their number was the treacherous one midway down, the one that bent like a bow at the slightest weight.

"Are you going down on your own or do I have to make you?"

The boy looked up at his father. The anger that had fueled him thus far was fading, seemingly sapped by the trip from the boy's bedroom. Instead, his father looked pained. If he didn't know better, he might think the Old Man was about to cry. But his father had said he was tired. *Dead tired.* And perhaps it was as simple as that.

"I'll go," the boy whispered, and he took the first tentative step down.

The change in temperature was immediate; it was like diving into a cold pool. He took another step down, and another.

He paused on the third step and looked back at his father. The bare bulb above paled the man's countenance. The grey circles under his eyes made him look like he'd been bludgeoned.

"Git!" the Old Man snarled. The boy went. When he reached the sagging step, he stopped, took a breath and leaped over it. His heel hit the lip of the next step, but the wood was damp, and the boy came down hard on his butt.

"Get some sleep. *And no more dreams.*"

As if he could help it.

His father closed the door, and the lock clicked. It would not open again until morning.

The boy descended the final few stairs and stepped onto the floor. Ice-cold cement sucked heat from his soles. He squinted, trying to adjust to the dark.

The usefulness of the light bulb ended a few feet into the basement. And there was no more source of light until he reached the...

The gears in his head ground to a halt, stopping short of allowing the dreaded name to be uttered.

He started picking out objects around him. The solemn metal face of the furnace, a stack of water softener salt bags, the frame of an old bicycle.

Straight ahead lay a distance of twenty or so feet before he'd come to a door. Three-quarters of that stretch was in pitch black. To get to the door, to get to the room, he had to dash through the darkness until his hand found the doorknob. Then, he would throw the door open, reach to his right, flip the wall switch and *presto.* An island of light in an ocean of black.

He girded himself for the sprint.

"One…two…"

He hesitated…but *why?* He'd already made this run two times this week. Both Monday and Thursday, he'd awakened screaming, bringing down the Old Man's wrath, and sending him here. To the penalty box. To time out. To the Night—

"Three!"

The boy startled at the sound of his own voice, and he lurched into motion. He hurtled into the darkness, his feet slapping the floor, echoing off the walls in hollow applause.

He bumped into something and spun, temporarily throwing himself and his inner compass off balance. He skidded across the floor and came to a stop.

Heart pounding in his chest, he quickly located the lit stairs off to his left. He made a rapid calculation and turned to face the invisible pathway to the room. He bolted, coming to a halt only when he slammed head-on into the door.

His hand floundered before finding the knob. He launched into his practiced routine. *Open door, flip switch, step inside.*

In seconds, the boy slipped into the room and slammed the door shut. A pink light overhead bathed him in imaginary warmth—he had made it.

He stepped back and sank into the waiting beanbag chair, facing the door. The small room with its mint green walls and rollaway bed felt almost welcoming, an odd feeling for a place that was meant as a punishment.

The boy pulled a quilt from the bed and wrapped it around him tight. For the first time in his life, he felt safe here in this room—in the Nightmare Room.

Because he hadn't bumped into something out there in the dark. He had bumped into *someone.*

He was almost certain of it.

He kept one eye on the door as the minutes hummed past on the illuminated clock on the nightstand. He busied himself with crayon and paper, doodling to keep his mind quiet. Soon, his vision began to flutter; the room began to strobe. And, in the space between two breaths, the boy sank into his beanbag chair and fell into a fitful sleep.

The doorknob twitched.

The boy bolted upright. He pressed back into the chair. His whole body started shivering, and he feared he would wet himself for the second time that night.

A thought…no, a *voice* crept into his head.

Coming in.

The door quivered as if someone was leaning against it, trying to stifle a laugh. Nails scratched against the wood.

"Dad?" the boy whispered.

The door shuddered.

"Is that you?" Knowing it was not.

Coming…

"Please don't."

Coming…

"No."

Coming…

"No!"

In.

CHAPTER 2

Peter smelled the town before he saw it—a rich, meaty musk that had always reminded him of Purina Dog Chow. Later in life, he would learn that it was the smell of burning skin and hair as workers blasted the pig carcasses with gas-guns. The Primeland pork processing plant employed a large number of Maple City residents. And saw thousands of hogs to their deaths.

Peter squinted as a semi approached in the opposite lane. It rushed past, causing the Ryder truck to rock and the old Prius it was towing to rock even more. Hannah stirred in the seat next to him but didn't wake. She had taken the long stretch through Indiana and around Chicago and had only turned over the wheel when she couldn't keep her eyes open just past Naperville.

He looked at her, slumped against the window, her loud Def Leppard t-shirt—a favorite of his—a glaring contrast to the woman who wore it. God, she was fetching, with her olive skin and the dark curls of hair she was never able to tame.

People always said Hannah didn't look her age, that she couldn't possibly be thirty. But the past weeks had taken their toll, and he thought his wife finally did look her age. Five years her senior, he could only imagine what *he* must look like.

Hannah snored as they rumbled into town with a substantially pared-down version of their earthly possessions crammed into the cargo section of the truck. They were pioneers, rolling in from the East in search of a brighter tomorrow.

We sure as hell could use one.

Peter tallied the number of dark yesterdays he and Hannah had accumulated these past few months.

He passed the sign stating *Welcome to Maple City! Home of...* and that was it. The rest of the greeting had been painted out. Up ahead, the first gas station appeared. Gas-4-U was lit up like Christmas, but the sign on the door said *Closed.*

"Good thing we filled up in the Quad Cities," he said aloud. Hannah mumbled and shifted in her seat.

Peter passed through the intersection—the crossroads between Routes 67 and 34—and headed into the city limits. Off to the left sat the old fashioned but well-kept Intermission Motor Lodge. The attached restaurant looked shuttered up, but the motel itself seemed to have a dozen or so reservations. The curtains of a lone window on the second floor flickered blue. Either someone couldn't sleep, or they had nodded off in front of the tube.

There used to be a large cow on top of the roof of the restaurant. A black Angus.

He crossed over the railroad tracks that cut a diagonal line through town, and he was on Main Street proper.

Their decision to move to Illinois had been made quickly. His sister had called about their father's downturn just a week ago, barely twenty-four hours after Hannah's Bad

Day. That's how life worked, wasn't it? Awful tended to cluster together.

He passed the First National Bank, and the clock by the fountain informed him that it was just after five o'clock. The sun wouldn't be up for another half hour, and their meeting with his dad's lawyer wasn't until eight.

A trip down memory lane? Why not?

He steered off Main and headed down Euclid Avenue, passing a hair salon, dry cleaners, a nail salon. It was sad. This block had once been populated with a candy store, a bookstore and a mom and pop office supply shop. It had moved on like most of the country—from the unique to the generic.

The town's founders had certainly done their job when naming the place. The streets were lined with maples—silver, sugars and the occasional red. In the predawn glow of the halogen streetlights, they stood standing watch over the avenues of Maple City, like onlookers at a parade. It was late August, and already a few of the trees were starting to show their fall colors. Giving up the ghost early this year.

On Oak Street, he hung a quick left. Something large shifted in the back of the truck, and he hoped that his Hush Room hadn't just done some major damage. The audio booth was portable, yes, but it was also heavy as hell. He made a mental note to go easy on the turns.

As they moved further into the neighborhood, Peter marveled at how much had changed. Gone were the dilapidated houses owned by the Brewsters and the Hollins—food stamp families with mean dogs and even meaner kids. In their place stood a row of college dorms. The campus was spreading. Good news for the college; bad news for the Brewsters and Hollins.

The sun was just starting to peek over the horizon as he parked the truck in front of 94 Oak Street.

At least it *hadn't changed.*

And yet it had. The lawn his father had always kept closely shorn was uneven. It had been mowed recently, that much was clear, but there had been no effort to trim around the trees, around the drain spouts. And Pop had always been careful to make horizontal passes across the lawn, leaving it as manicured as a golf course. It was the work of a kid trying to get the job done as fast as possible.

The house itself was still in fine order—no peeling paint, no hanging gutters. But the state of the lawn brought on a wave of loneliness that Peter couldn't weather alone.

"We're here," he said, gently nudging Hannah. "All ashore that's going ashore."

His wife wrinkled her nose, opened her eyes and yawned. "We're here?"

* * *

Peter fished the spare key from underneath a ceramic frog sporting a fishing pole and opened the door.

"Oh, no," Hannah said, putting her hand over her nose. "That's bad. I mean *bad* bad."

The stink of rot hit Peter's nose like a sledgehammer. The house was hot inside, and the combo of heat and decay was hellacious.

"We're going to have to fumigate the place before we move in," Hannah said as she forced open a window. "What the hell is that?"

"I'll go check," he said, slipping past her. "Would you take a look at the thermostat? It's got to be a hundred degrees in here."

He walked down the hall, past his mothers' collection of framed doilies hanging on the walls. He took a quick peek into the half bathroom—he wished he hadn't.

Peter stopped short of the kitchen, his foot poised over the linoleum floor.

"Oh, God."

The entire contents of the freezer had been emptied and laid out on the kitchen table. A mountain of pork chops sweltered inside ballooning ziplock bags. A carton of Whitey's chocolate ice cream—his father's favorite—sat in a dried brown puddle. Scattered bags of corn, vegetable medley and peas completed the picture.

"I turned it down!" Hannah called from the other room. "It was set at eighty-four."

"Don't come in here," he replied, venturing closer to the mess. One of the ziplock bags had burst, exposing a stack of pork chops to the air. White maggots wriggled across the surface of the grey meat. "Not unless you want to lose your lunch."

"I haven't even had breakfast," she countered, but she stayed put.

Suppressing his rising gorge, Peter opened the cupboard, fished out a box of trash bags and got to work.

* * *

After detaching the Prius from the truck, Peter and Hannah spun past a gas station, filled the tank and arrived at the Heartland Diner just before eight. When the menus came, neither of them had much of an appetite.

"Share a cinnamon roll?" Peter asked.

"Sounds good."

They placed their order with an overworked waitress and sat back with their coffee.

Hannah glanced about the diner, taking in the farmhands in the corner, the church ladies at the big center table and the cop at the counter. Big breakfasts all around.

"I like the house," she said. "It's bigger than I remember. And nicer. Well, except for the…"

"The kitchen from Hell?"

Hannah grinned. How long had it been since he'd seen that grin? "When are we going to see your dad?"

"Let's settle our business with Mr. Moots and then we'll swing by the home."

"His name is really Mr. Moots?"

"Gary Moots, yes, ma'am."

The cinnamon roll came and Hannah dove for it. Peter let her have the whole thing.

"Everything's going to be okay, right, Peter?"

He took a long sip of coffee. "It is."

"You promise?"

"I do."

The diner door opened, and a portly man sporting a bushy mustache and a brown suit entered. He was carrying a battered briefcase.

Hannah leaned into Peter. "A hundred bucks that's Moots."

She was right.

"You folks the Larsons?" the big man boomed, flashing a toothy smile.

"Guilty," Hannah said.

"Guilty! That's funny." He offered her his beefy hand. "Gary Moots. And you're Hannah?"

"Pleased to meet you, Mr. Moots."

"You must be Peter."

"Thanks for meeting us." He sat next to Hannah, letting Mr. Moots sit opposite them in the booth. It was a tight fit for the lawyer.

"You should get a skillet," Mr. Moots said. "Ham scramble, corned beef hash, home fries. They make a mean skillet."

He looks like a walrus. A walrus who loves skillets.

The man flagged down the waitress. "I'll have what they're having."

"A cinnamon roll?" the waitress asked, her arms weighted down with plates of pancakes.

"No, just the coffee." He turned back to Peter. "Your dad set this all up in advance, so this should be a relatively simple process. You've been out to see him?"

"Not yet."

"Nice place, Applegate. I've got a lot of clients out there. Good outfit. Great food. They lay out a Sunday buffet that's top notch. As good as anything you'd get here. Bacon, eggs, sausage—the works."

Peter's stomach rumbled, recalling the spoiled meat in his parents' kitchen. "Can you give me a little more info about what happened? My sister is incommunicado, and the woman I talked to from your office didn't have a lot of details."

"I can only tell you what the home told me. The gal from Meals on Wheels found him in quite a state. Not your typical fluster, mind you, more of a panic. Couldn't calm him down. After that, I don't really...see, your dad's case wasn't specifically mine. I'm sure they'll have a lot more information for you at the home."

Mr. Moots cracked open his briefcase and shuffled through papers. His search continued for some time, accompanied by a series of unconscious grunts. Hannah glanced at Peter, threatening to break into yet another grin.

"I'm sorry, folks. I'm working out of my car at the moment. My partner up and left town with our secretary a couple of days ago. After twenty years, you think you know a person." Triumphantly, he pulled a folder from the case. "Ah! Here we go."

He laid the folder open on the table. The waitress returned with his coffee.

"Okay, so, like I said, your dad's set. They've got him in a room with your mom. They do that sometimes out there at Applegate. Keep the couples together when they can. Like I said, they're a good outfit. Anywhoo, he's set. He worked this all up in advance."

"That's great," Peter said, then added, "I mean, that it's going to be so simple."

Mr. Moots slapped the folder shut. "So, loose ends. Just a few. I've already got some nibbles on the house—sight unseen—so it's great you're here in town. I'm no realtor, so I'll introduce you to Lillian Dann. Do you know the Danns? Nice folks. Her husband Bob works over at the True Value. Lillian can help you get the place cleared out and get it listed right away. Might as well strike while the iron's hot."

Peter frowned. "What do you mean, nibbles?"

"Potential buyers. Like I said, I'm no realtor, but word gets around, and I start getting calls. With its proximity to the college, I'd be surprised if their business office didn't put in an offer."

"But we'll be staying in the house, Mr. Moots," Hannah said.

"Oh?" The lawyer cocked his head. "So, you've decided to buy it?"

"No." Peter felt his face go flush. Hannah gripped his hand under the table. "Your office told me that we were good to move in. My wife and I…we're here to move in."

The lawyer grew flustered, almost spilling his coffee. "My office said that? Who said that?"

"I'm not sure. A woman."

Mr. Moot's face went white. "Was it Ms. Eagleton?"

"That sounds familiar."

The man put the folder back in his case, then pulled it back out, unsure of his next move. "Folks, unless you want to buy the house, it's got to be liquidated. Applegate gets paid out of the proceeds. My secretary—that is, Ms. Eagleton—

should never have led you to believe..." He shook his head. "She let things fall through the cracks before she took off with Willem. She let things fall through the cracks."

Peter saw red. "Are you telling us that we drove halfway across the country and now—"

Hannah put a hand on his shoulder. "Calm down, Peter."

"I'm sorry," the lawyer muttered.

"What do you suggest we do, Mr. Moots?" Peter asked.

The man swallowed hard. "I think you should go see your father."

* * *

Hannah sat in the car holding a to-go container while Peter paced outside in the parking lot behind the diner, willing his little sister to pick up the phone. After the fourth call, she finally did.

"Peter—"

"They're selling the house, Gina."

"What? Why?"

Peter gritted his teeth. "To cover his expenses. How could you not know that? How could you not tell me?"

"Dad took care of everything himself. He didn't want a big mess like after Mom...he arranged it all himself."

"Well, he bungled the whole thing. Hannah and I thought we were good to go, and now we're stuck here with everything we own..."

"Oh, God..."

"...and now this Moots fellow says we're up shit's creek."

"You shouldn't have… All I did was sign the papers the nursing home Fedexed."

A scarecrow of a cook slipped out the back door for a smoke, but one glare from Peter sent him scurrying back inside.

"We've got our hands full out here, Peter. We've been taking care of Dave's sister's kids ever since her husband ran off. I've got reports due, and Dave's got corporate from Iowa City coming in—"

"I've been pretty damn busy myself if you recall."

Silence on the other end. "How is Hannah?"

"She'd be a hell of a lot better if we had a place to stay," Peter said and ended the call.

He hopped into the car.

"What's the plan, Mr. Larson?" Hannah asked.

"Not sure yet."

"But you're working on it?"

"I am."

Peter's phone vibrated—probably his sister texting to apologize. But the incoming text was from Mika at Flatiron Audio.

PDFs of your first three books are up on the FTP let production know when you're going to start recording thanks.

"Who's that?" Hannah asked.

Peter sighed. "Work. They're nipping at my heels."

"When do you need to start?"

"ASAP." Peter flipped on the windshield wipers and watched as dead bugs danced in the blue wiper fluid. "What do you say we go get this over with?"

CHAPTER 3

Applegate was out on the north edge of town, along with the town's only hospital, the YMCA and a couple of auto body shops. It was a nondescript, one-story brick building that sprawled across the landscape, sectioned off in multiple wings. Behind it stretched farmland as far as the eye could see.

Peter soured at the sight of it.

Hannah was watching him closely. "How long has it been since you've seen your mom?"

"Almost a year, I think. Great visit. Half the time she was screaming at me, the other half she was screaming at someone else. And *I* was the only other person in the room."

Hannah rubbed his neck. "Still—"

"Still *nothing*, hon. I put in my time with that woman. Your mom and my mom? Like night and day. I'm only here because of Pop."

Peter turned down the drive leading to the home. A member of the grounds crew stood in the middle of the road filling a pothole. He took a drag on his cigarette and grudgingly stepped aside and waved them past.

"Are you...prepared to see him?"

"What do you mean?"

"You know. Like *this*."

Peter steered toward visitors parking.

"We don't even know what *this* is yet."

But that was a lie. As Peter was locking up the house on Oak Street, his folks' neighbor Mrs. Nathan had stopped by to chat.

"So sad. *So* sad," she had said. "Always such a nice man. He fixed my Robert's lawnmower, you know? For free, God bless him. To see him like that. Never heard a curse out of your father until that day. The things he said to those paramedics. Dear me!"

She had gone on to describe the history of his slow, downhill decline—one which had ended with Bill Larson being taken away in an ambulance as his lifelong neighbors watched. Listening to the woman's chronology, Peter had realized that he couldn't have been there for his father even if he had known. He'd had his hands full. He was back east trying to hold his own world together while his father's was falling apart.

"Peter?"

He roused, realizing that he had already parked—the Prius's gas engine gone silent as the electric kicked in.

"Are you going to be okay?"

"I don't have much of a choice, do I?" he snapped, instantly regretting it.

"I'm right here with you, you big dope."

"Okay."

Hannah snuggled close. "Right here."

* * *

After checking in at the front desk, Peter and Hannah made their way down the hall to the dementia ward. They passed the day room where a middle-aged man with a stiff toupee hosted a karaoke session. A cluster of elderly women in wheelchairs surrounded him—the world's oldest groupies. The man belted out Sinatra like there was no tomorrow.

Hannah took his hand and laced her fingers in his. She'd never been here to the home because that's the way he wanted it.

An old fellow with a bowed back zipped out in front of them in his wheelchair. "Beep beep!" he cried.

"Back to your room, Reggie," a nurse called, but Reggie was already wheeling it down the hall.

Go, Reggie, go.

Following the front desk's directions, they skirted past a clutch of women watching Fox News on the small TV at the nurses' station and stepped into D Ward.

D for dementia. A little on the nose, isn't it?

Hannah squeezed his hand and brought him back to attention.

This wing of the home was quite different. There were no residents out in the hallway, save for a young man with Down Syndrome wearing a Star Wars sweatshirt and standing vigil next to the wall-mounted hand sanitizer dispenser.

A tall, black orderly sauntered down the hall, ignoring the young man's attempt at a high five. Hannah approached him.

"We're looking for Room 16? Bill and Myrna Larson."

The man pointed to a room behind him and kept going, never missing a stride.

As Peter passed the man in the sweatshirt, he offered up his hand. "High five?" This time, he was the one who was ignored.

"Here," Hannah said, and stepped back, allowing Peter to enter first.

Peter paused just inside the room. It was sparse. There were no pictures on the walls, no knickknacks on the dressers. The first bed was made but empty—his mother's. On the second sat William P. Larson.

Peter couldn't move.

His wife walked past him and approached the old fellow. "Hello, Papa Larson. It's Hannah." She took his frail hand in hers and gave it a rub.

"Hannah Banana?" His voice was dry as toast.

Bill Larson had always been a big, hearty fellow—the kind of guy people called jolly. But the years reduced him to almost nothing.

"Come say hello to your dad," Hannah urged.

Reluctantly, Peter went to his father's side. The man needed a shave. He'd mention that to the nurses.

"Hey Pop." His voice broke, and he tried again. "It's Pete. You're looking real…" He couldn't finish. He turned and dropped onto the other bed, opposite his father.

"We brought you a cinnamon roll from the diner," Hannah said, holding the Styrofoam container out to him. "Peter says they're your favorite."

The man stared at the offering. "No, that's not mine."

"Yes it is," said Hannah. "We got it for you."

Peter's father looked worried. "I'm so sorry. I don't have my wallet."

"It's okay, Pop," Peter said, his voice tight.

The old man stood up and instantly sat back down. He searched his pockets. "No, I didn't…I've been meaning to get more organized…" He shook his head as if to jar his thoughts loose. "That's mine, you say?"

Hannah opened the container and showed him the cinnamon roll. His whole demeanor changed.

"Ah! That looks good. You make that?"

"No, Pop," Hannah cooed. "It's from the diner. Peter bought it for you, didn't you, Peter?" She was forcing him into the conversation, and he resented her for it.

"Peter," his father said, his smile straining as he searched for the next thing to say. "Pete…?"

Hannah took the old man's hand and gave it a rub. Something about the gesture lit up Peter's memory, and before he could block it out, he saw his wife standing over another hospital bed, holding another trembling hand.

Stop it.

The puff of oxygen.

No.

The IV drip.

No!

"Get off my bed!" a voice shrieked.

Peter leaped to his feet and whirled about. Standing in the doorway was a shrunken woman in a baby blue house dress. She was shaking her cane at him and scowling.

Jesus, it's Bette Davis.

But of course, it wasn't—it was Myrna Larson.

"Get out of my room!"

"It's me, Mom."

Peter and his mother had never been the closest of friends—quite the contrary. He was a boy, and boys were messy. Many were the night that Myrna Larson forced him to dust or mop or vacuum away the dirt he brought into her life. His father, bless him, would always reward him for these episodes by inviting him to the garage to listen to the Cubs on the radio and to enjoy an ice-cold Coke.

What are you doing in my room!" his mother screamed.

Just past the raging woman, Peter spotted the young man in the Star Wars sweatshirt trying to catch a glimpse of the action.

Peter took a step forward, hands out. His mother took a swing at him with her cane.

"Easy, Peter," Hannah said.

"Mom, it's me. It's Peter. Your son."

"You're not my son!" the woman roared and took another swing. This time, she clipped his hand.

The man in the sweatshirt darted into the room and planted himself firmly in between Peter and his mother. "No!" he huffed, literally putting his foot down. "No!"

The old woman patted the fellow on his shoulder. "Thank you. Oh, my. Thank you."

The stubborn, tubby man locked eyes with Peter and pointed an accusing finger. "No."

Peter felt an uncomfortable rush of anger toward the guy.

"Hey, Skywalker—"

"Peter," Hannah urged. "Stop."

23

"Why don't you—"

Hannah yanked him back, forcing him to face her. "What the hell are you thinking?"

A matronly nurse appeared at the door. "You're on the wrong wing, Ronnie. Leave these people be." She coaxed the young man from the room. Ronnie went, but not before flipping Peter double birds.

"Peter?"

Peter turned to see his mother staring at him, her face a picture of sheer bafflement.

"When did you get here?"

* * *

Two nurses and a woman from administration—who kept referring to his mother as Mrs. Logan—gave Peter and Hannah the lowdown on Peter's father's intake, condition and prognosis. He had come in screaming but had settled down considerably since.

"Is this a passing thing or not?" Peter asked—his only question.

The woman from administration's answer was short and sweet. "Not."

After allowing the woman to give them a perfunctory tour of the place, Peter and Hannah took their leave of Applegate. The fresh air brought welcome relief.

Peter paused before turning the key in the ignition.

"You all right?" Hannah asked, her eyes trying to find his.

"I just had a big wave of lonely wash over me. Not loneliness, just...*lonely*. Like I don't want to stay, and I don't want to leave."

"I feel the lonely too."

"Fuck it," Peter said as he turned the ignition. "You wanted to know the plan, Mrs. Larson? Well, here's the plan."

Hannah raised an eyebrow. "You got the plan?"

"We swing by the house, grab the truck, call the Ryder office to buy ourselves an extra day or two, find a place to stay for the night, grab ourselves a hard, hard drink and then..."

"And then?"

Peter threw the car into reverse. "Let's get that far first."

CHAPTER 4

The Intermission Motor Lodge turned out to be both pleasant and accommodating. Not only was there a room available on the top floor—Peter couldn't stand listening to people tromp above all night—but they could check in right away.

"I don't understand why places make people wait if their room is ready," the woman behind the counter said. She wore paint-spattered coveralls, and her hair hung down in wisps from underneath a paper hat. "There's probably a good reason for that, but until I figure it out, what the hey."

Peter parked the truck while Hannah parked the Prius. Their room was in the back, away from the road, and he and Hannah took the cement steps to the second floor.

The room was tidy, if small. The walls had a fresh coat of paint, and there were extra pillows in the closet. A flyer by the phone touted the motel as the perfect place for families to stay during graduation.

Hannah tossed Peter the TV remote. "I call dibs on the shower."

Peter clicked on the weather channel. The Carolinas were getting the brunt of Hurricane Elmer.

He heard Hannah turn on the shower, heard her hoot at the water temperature. He thought about waiting until he was certain she was well into her shampooing routine and then slipping into the shower with her, but they hadn't crossed that bridge yet. Their love life would return—he was sure of that—but best not to rush it. Better to settle the current mess first and then take it from there.

Dad looked so old.

His phone chirped, and he scrubbed the thought from his mind. He checked the caller ID. It was Moots.

"Mr. Larson?"

"What can I do for you, Mr. Moots?"

"I've been going through your father's paperwork. Willem, my partner, he left things in quite a state. Anywhoo, ever since this morning, I've been piecing things together. I called up Lillian Dann, and we sorted it out. I felt real bad about our meeting this morning, you know, just awful. Usually, I'm so organized, but like I said, this whole business with Willem and Ms. Eagleton—"

"Was there something, in particular, you wanted to tell me, Mr. Moots?"

"Yes, sorry," the lawyer said. "It's about the other property."

"What other property?"

"See, Ms. Eagleton wasn't half wrong when she told you that you could move right in. She just didn't...well, she might have gotten confused about the arrangement, what with planning to leave town and all. They won't answer their phones, can you believe that? Either of them."

"What other property, Mr. Moots?"

"The farmhouse. The one your dad bought at auction."

* * *

Thirty minutes later, Peter and Hannah were zipping away from the motel.

Hannah rolled down the window and let her hair dry in the breeze.

"You think we'll ever own a car that has working air conditioning?"

Peter smirked. "Hope springs eternal."

He'd had to put the location into his phone to map the way; as a kid, he'd never had much reason to venture south of the train tracks. The phrase 'other side of the tracks' certainly applied to Maple City. This was where mobile homes muscled-out houses, where campaign signs remained in yards long after the election and every neighborhood had its own bar.

After passing Kellum's Salvage, they reached the city limits where dirt roads replaced asphalt. Soon, the car was kicking up dust as Maple City receded in the rearview mirror.

Hannah pointed out a prefab building with a large, rustic railroad tie cross in front. A hand-painted sign proclaimed it to be The Lord's Harvest Church. "You think they speak in tongues?"

"Probably. And handle snakes, too."

"Snakes?"

"Probably."

Peter's phone informed him of an upcoming turn, and he took it. Fields of feed corn flanked them on either side.

"A whole lotta nuthin'," Hannah offered in her best Midwestern twang.

"Welcome to Illinois."

A patch of trees appeared in the distance, mirage-like and lush. Peter hoped for the best and was rewarded when his phone guided him the way of the foliage.

As they turned up the gravel drive, a sour taste came into Peter's mouth. He tapped the brake a bit too hard, causing the car to cough.

"Peter?"

Perhaps it was the size of the place or the vacant windows that stared down like dead eyes. Whatever it was, Peter disliked the house immediately.

Lillian Dann was waiting for them in her bright orange Mini Cooper.

"Hey, you two!" she crooned. "Let me show you around."

* * *

Lillian Dann was a pint-sized woman full of energy and positivity poised atop of a pair of ridiculously high heels. The sound of those heels tapping across the foyer floor brought to mind the clicking nails of a nervous dachshund.

"Such a spacious entrance!" the realtor cooed. "Think of the parties you could throw in this house."

Peter looked around. The entranceway was littered with leaves, empty beer cans, an empty box of condoms. *Looks like someone's already beat us to it.*

Before him, a sagging staircase split the room, leading up to the second floor. The left banister remained intact; the right hung halfway off, missing scores of balusters. Like a broken jaw. There was evidence someone had attempted to repair it, but the fix didn't seem to have taken.

"Old Mootsy felt *so* bad about the mix-up," the realtor said. "He's a good man in a tough situation. When he asked if I'd show you around, I said, 'Of course, Mootsy! Anything for you, sweetie.'"

Hannah squeezed Peter's hand.

"Is it safe to walk in here?" she asked, eyeing a large crack in the floorboards.

"You bet!" Lillian crowed. And to prove her point, she began hopping up and down. Dust rose from the floor. "These old farmhouses were built to last. Old school carpentry, solid foundations. Good bones. They knew how to make 'em back then!" Hop, hop, hop.

She's going to break her ankles doing that.

"What about water?" Peter asked. "Electricity?"

Lillian grinned and nodded toward the light switch next to him. "Give it a try."

Peter flipped the switch, and a lone bare bulb flickered on above their heads.

"I pulled a few strings," the realtor said, seeming quite proud of herself. "My Bobby's cousin works at Sauk Electric. Got you back on the grid. You may need to replace a few outlets here and there, but that's to be expected. Your dad did a good job fixing the place up. Good enough to rent, anyway. The plumbing is solid, and you've got your own well out back. I tell you, this house is move-in ready."

Move-in ready? Peter eyeballed the stained ceiling staring through a single coat of paint. That was his father, all right. He had never been detail-oriented when it came to fixing things. His car wash was notorious for having hoses that were more duct tape than rubber.

"When did my father buy this place?"

The realtor flipped through her notepad. "It was purchased twenty years ago at public auction. He had it set up as a rental. Brought in steady income until a couple of months ago. It's almost as if this was meant to be!"

Peter looked around at the dilapidated place. If this were fate, as the woman seemed to imply, he'd have to have a chat with the head office.

"The rent covered the taxes, paid for the upkeep. Most of the renters were itinerant workers if you know what I mean. Mexicans." Lillian said the word in a hushed, conspiratorial tone that made Peter squirm.

"I don't understand," Peter said. "Mr. Moots wants my folks' house sold lickety-split. Why not this place?"

The realtor referred to her paperwork. "The house is actually owned by Larson Enterprises."

Larson Enterprises was a big name for a little concern that consisted of two storage units, a car wash and a suntan shop. But Bill Larson had divested all his holdings. Or so Peter had assumed.

"It's excluded from his Medicaid eligibility as it's part of a business property essential to self-support," Lillian Dann rattled off. "As long as it's rented, it stays in the family."

"So, we'd have to rent this place? From my father?"

The realtor flashed a sly smile. "How does a dollar a month sound?"

"Sounds fishy," Peter said.

"All on the up and up," Lillian said. "And *if* you decide later on to work up a little financing and make it official, I'd be happy to help you out with the paperwork."

Hannah elbowed Peter in the ribs. "Can you imagine what this place would go for back east?"

"I can also imagine the taxes."

Lillian held up a finger and quickly searched her papers. "Speaking of taxes, it does look like your father is a tad behind. Nothing we can't sort out."

"How much does he owe?" Peter asked.

Lillian brightened. "That's the good news. Seeing as it's just outside the city limits—and a fixer-upper—five hundred should cover it."

This place isn't even worth that in wood and nails.

"Follow me! I've got lots to show you. Lots!" The realtor took off down the left hallway, leaving Peter and Hannah standing in the foyer.

"Oh, my God," Hannah whispered.

"That woman's selling it like she's actually...selling it."

"Oh...my...God," Hannah repeated.

"I know, right?"

"This place is *amazing*."

Peter blinked. "What?"

Hannah clutched his arm. "This is just like my show, *It's Broken, You Buy It*. You know, the one you erased from the DVR."

"I didn't erase it."

"All of season two. You did, I know you did, but that's not the point." She was positively beaming. "This is *that* kind of house. A broken place we can put back together. I just know it is. I just know it."

Peter wanted to burst her bubble right there in the foyer before they had even seen the rest of the house. In his mind, he had already started the calculations. He'd have to check the foundation, check the roof, repair that banister and God knows what else.

But he didn't. He stayed silent and wondered at the spark in his wife's eyes.

"Did I lose you?" Lillian Dann's voice echoed from the hall. "Come on; I want to show you the kitchen. But put your imagination caps on first!"

"Go on," Peter said and nodded toward the hallway. Hannah grinned a full-faced grin and bounded away. He was alone.

Peter scuffed his shoe on the floor. He carefully drew a circle in the dust with the tip of his shoe. Then he sketched in two dots for eyes. He paused before adding the mouth. Smiley face or sad? He left it blank.

He could hear Hannah and Lillian talking down the hall but couldn't make out what they were saying. No doubt, the realtor was ingratiating herself with his wife, smoothing over whatever damage might have been done by Moots. The woman was good at her job; he had to give her that. The fact that she could present this shithole as if it were Caesars Palace while standing in piles of mouse turds had won her a modicum of his respect.

She's going to have to fumigate those high heels of hers when she gets home.

Grey was the predominant color of the house—grey walls, grey floors, grey mood. It was a utilitarian place, of that he was certain. A plain house for people who did honest work. No room for frivolity. Whatever ghosts might haunt this place would no doubt shrink in horror at the midnight shenanigans of the local teenagers who spent their illicit Saturday nights here.

Hannah had gotten it wrong. This was not the sort of house featured on her home improvement show; this was every house in every horror movie he'd ever seen.

"Hello-oo, Mrs. Bates," he called. The only reply was his wife's distant laughter.

When had the place been built? The twenties? The thirties? And it was still standing; he had to give it that. In fact, the only real overt evidence of its decline was the staircase. The way it tilted. And that banister. What in the world had caused that?

He walked up to the staircase and mounted the first few steps. He shook the intact banister, but it held firm. Then, he gave the broken banister a kick, and it swayed out and back. Out and back.

Peter turned around a full circle, taking in the view from his elevated vantage point. It would take days—no... weeks, months—to get this bad boy into shape, but he had to admit it seemed more plausible from up here.

He thought about heading up to the second floor but reconsidered. Plenty of time for that later. Besides, who knew what he might find up there. The mummified corpse of a squatter? A nest of rabid raccoons? Best not to go it alone.

He tromped back down to the foyer. Instead of following after Hannah and Lillian, he opted for the second hallway, the one to the right of the staircase. He crept past what looked to be a wadded-up pair of underwear—this place had been quite the teenage brothel—and continued down the hall. He passed a large, empty side room with heavy, maroon curtains and imagined the pleasure he'd feel pulling the ghastly things down, letting in the light.

The end of the hallway opened up into a back room that looked out across the yard. A small pond lined with cattails lay a stone's throw from the house, and beyond it a large, green harvester worked a field of soybeans, kicking up dust.

He felt a sudden itch and slapped the back of his neck. Damn mosquitoes. Once you feel their bite, it's too late.

Peter spied a lone child's boot sitting next to the back door, toppled over on its side. He reached down and picked it up. It felt small and familiar in his hand.

Stop it, Daddy! Tickling is torture!

Grief exploded in his chest. He sank to the floor, gripping the boot to him. Invisible bands of pressure squeezed his ribs inward, and he groaned.

Michael.

He tried to shove the memory away—the boy in the bed, his little pink feet, his fingers dancing across them causing the boy to giggle and kick.

No!

Another memory took its place—the last time he and Hannah had made love, her lying heavy atop him, her tears landing hot on his neck. And whispering to him. Whispering *his* name.

Michael!

Peter tossed the boot aside.

He took a deep breath, coughing at the harsh intake of stale air. He stood up fast, and the room seemed to pulse, a trick of pressure behind his eyes. He clenched them shut.

When he opened them again, he was facing a narrow, grey door. A basement door.

His vision had steadied and the room no longer moved about him. But the door…

It's breathing.

CHAPTER 5

Peter's legs buckled, his sense of equilibrium not yet returned. The door, of course, was not breathing, but then again, neither was he. It was simply acting in concert with a door opened across the house by Hannah or Lillian Dann, the draft causing the two doors to move in sympathy.

He grasped the doorknob and pulled the door open. A belch of fetid air hit his nostrils, causing him to recoil. A wooden staircase descended into the darkness—a rickety invitation. Like the rest of the house, it sagged and bowed.

The third step down stood apart from the rest. Instead of faded grey, it was pale and unpainted. No effort had been made to match the rest of the stairs, and again Peter recognized his father's handiwork.

He flicked the switch next to the banister, and a camera-burst of white lit up the basement before the bulb died. The flash afforded Peter a momentary glimpse of the full stretch of the staircase, from the top to the foot. No gaps. Good.

Peter pulled his phone, tapped on the LED light and placed a tentative toe on the first step. It responded with a groan. It felt springy but not dangerously so. He swallowed and took the next step. And the next. Soon, he was standing on the cement floor of the crypt-cool basement.

"Olly olly oxen free," he called. No response, not even the squeak and scurry of a rat.

Training his small light about the room, the only thing he found remotely frightening was the sheer amount of clutter that had accumulated. It was a hoarder's heaven and a picker's hell—strewn plywood sheets, three-legged chairs, broken panes of glass. The useless detritus of generations.

Thanks a lot, Dad.

Peter was surprised at his anger, and he hated himself for it. His father's only fault was growing old. He instantly wished he had given the man a hug the second he saw him, wished had held his hand like Hannah. She was the one who always knew the right thing to do—when to share a word or a touch or a glance to soften the moment.

Him? He hadn't even looked the man in the eyes.

"I'm so sorry. I don't have my wallet."

Peter winced, remembering his father's fumbling. Bill Larson, 'Big Bear' Larson as his friends called him, had always had the gift of the gab. A gregarious guy, his father was a man who got an invite to every barbeque. Granted, he had been a formidable grill master with his shiny tongs and *Kiss the Cook* apron, but it was his company they sought even more than his ribs.

When Peter was thirteen, Mr. Porter, a family friend, had pulled him aside at his 4th of July cookout. At first, Peter thought the man had spied him trying to sneak into his garage, where it was rumored he had a fridge filled with ice-cold Falstaff beer. But no such thing.

"Your dad's a good man, Peter," Mr. Porter had said, his Hawaiian shirt ablaze in the July sun. "When they laid me off from Primeland, he put in a good word for me at his job. I was working alongside him that very next week. If it weren't for him, I never would have bought my tow truck, never have the business I have today. He'll never mention it, so I am. That's the kind of man your dad is."

Peter kicked a pile of rusted rebar, sending them scattering. He didn't need a stranger to tell him what a good man his father was. He had lived it. When his mother was off her meds and on the warpath, it was Big Bear Larson who'd protected him, who had made him feel like everything was going to be okay. He'd promised Hannah that very same thing this morning. But he was not his father. He wasn't even half the man—not even half the father.

"I'm no one's father," he said to the empty room.

Something in the statement's bluntness, in its utter honesty, woke him from his reverie. It was true. He wasn't a father anymore. But maybe, he could take another crack at being a son.

A leaning tower of cardboard boxes in the corner next to the utility sink caught his eye. His father's trademark scrawl adorned each and every one.

Speak of the devil.

Peter maneuvered past a stack of crumbling drywall and shined the light on the boxes. They were variously labeled *Taxes, Receipts* and *Personal*. He flipped opened the top of the first box—the cardboard dissolved in his hand like flaking skin.

As advertised, the boxes contained records of businesses past, bills accrued, debts paid. He was more interested in those marked *Personal*. And of course, they were at the bottom of the heap.

As he dragged down the upper boxes and set them down, creating a reverse version of the tower, he wondered at their being here. More than likely, his father had moved them to this basement when he gave up his office on the square and the storage units. His mother *hated* clutter, hated mess. She liked precision and routine and was thrown off course by so much as a cabinet door left ajar.

"*Peter! Bill! Close the GD cabinets! You men. You GD men!*"

He didn't know then what he knew now. That his mother's mean streak had a name and that it could be tempered by medication. No wonder his father had brought his messy, *man* business to this basement where it could spread out without fear of reprisal.

The bottommost boxes had been crushed by the weight of those above. Peter unfolded the crisscrossed top panels and gazed within.

His sister's toothy grin stared up at him through cracked glass. It was her high school graduation photo, and Peter swore she had never looked happier. Happy to get out of town, no doubt. Out from under Mom. Gina suffered her moods differently than he and his father had. His mother made his sister her confidant, tried to pit her against the males in the house.

"*We know, don't we, Gina? You and I? Men are dogs. They're filthy dogs.*"

Her effort hadn't worked. It had only driven Gina away, leaving his mother alone with *that man*.

Poor Dad.

Peter sorted through the rest of the contents. There were a few unframed photos of himself from when he was a teen, baby Gina holding a stuffed giraffe, a candid shot of his mother and father at an ice cream social. His father was laughing; his mother was not.

The remaining items in the *Personal* boxes were his father's various ribbons for barbeque excellence, a plaque from the Rotary Club and an assortment of pen sets and desk calendars. And that was it—a sparse collection.

He set these boxes atop the others for later and realized that in doing so, he had already begun to believe that there *would* be a later. Hannah was on a trajectory after months of stagnation. Who was he to stop it?

Clink.

Peter turned. The sound came again, the clink of metal on metal. Peter raised his phone and swept the basement.

Nothing.

Clink.

He pinpointed the direction of the noise and headed that way. Back into the bowels of the basement, past a rack of shovels and rakes, past stacks of paint cans and coils of garden hose.

His light fell on a door.

Peter had to move closer to confirm what had at first seemed a trick of his eyes—there were deep scratch marks dug into the wood.

The gouges were high up on the door, ruling out the scrabbling work of an animal. And they were spaced evenly, suggesting they were made by…

A hand.

A combination lock held the door tight.

"What the hell?" Peter whispered.

Suddenly, the lock twitched in place, clinking against the latch.

He grabbed the lock. It was cold to the touch. He spun the dial back and forth and gave it a yank. It held.

Breathing heavily, Peter walked back to the pile of rebar, grabbed one of the rusted rods, slipped it through the lock's metal U and forced it down hard.

CHAPTER 6

The door swung open. The boy grit his teeth, catching the edge of his tongue in the process. His mouth filled with the taste of copper.

He swallowed the bloody saliva quickly, sensing that whatever was coming in could smell it. *Might want it.*

Coming in.

The boy balled his fists and prepared for the worst.

Instead, he watched as the door opened fully, revealing nothing but the basement beyond. Still, his adrenaline was flowing, and it gave him a frantic, temporary bravery.

"Come on in, then!" he shouted. "Come in, come in, come in, if you want to. Shut up and…come…in!"

A whiff of smoke tickled his nose—the smell of cheap firecrackers, like sparklers. Like the black snakes kids lit on the playground, their bodies growing and spitting ash and smoke.

Like sulfur.

I will. I am.

All of the air seemed to leave the room at once like the sudden exhale before a tornado. The lamp dimmed, and the boy's skin turned electric. The walls began to vibrate, driving its tattoo deep into his gut.

The room turned grainy, clouded. The boy's eyes hurt. Red swirls swam at the periphery of his vision as if he were about to cry blood. He squinted, willing himself away. Anywhere, just…away.

Something blew past his head with a rush of air and a clatter of claws.

The boy slowly opened his eyes. And what he saw in the sparse light made his stomach twist.

A shadow swirled above his head. It circled him, swimming in the air, leaving inky tendrils behind. It moved like liquid fire, cold and black, nails clicking against the walls as it circled lower and lower. As it did so, the boy made out two, dull grey eyes. Flatworm eyes.

"What are you?" the boy whispered, feeling the hair on his scalp prickle.

The darkness chittered in reply.

I am Whisper. I am Mr. Tell.

The boy's blood howled in his veins. He turned, following the molten movement of the thing.

"What do you tell?"

The thing cackled a crackling fire chuckle as it whished past. Closer this time.

Secrets. S-s-s-s-secrets.

The shadow brushed against him, numbing him to the bone. The boy instinctively pushed the thing away—its icy nothingness flowed through his fingers like sleet.

"What secrets?"

Its eyes brightened, and it circled faster, leaving black stains in the air. The room thrummed and darkened in its wake.

Mr. Tell! Mr. Tell! Mr. Tell! Mr. Tell!

"What do you tell?" he cried. "What do you tell?"

The thing stopped short and rose up in front of him like a king cobra. Its dead eyes bore into his.

Who's a good boy?

Not the thing's voice, but another. A warm voice. A woman's voice.

"Mama?"

Mr. Tell opened his horrid, black mouth and struck.

CHAPTER 7

"Peter!"

"Christ!" Peter cried. He dropped the rebar, and it hit the floor with a jarring clang.

He turned to find Hannah standing in the doorway to the small room, her head tilted in puzzlement. "Nervous much?"

"I…"

"I've been calling you for five minutes. Don't tell me you didn't hear me."

"I didn't."

Hannah gave the rebar a nudge with her foot. "Is that your weapon? Don't tell me there are mice down here. What did you do with it? Did you bash one? No! Don't tell me." Hannah could deal with a lot—had dealt with a lot—but anything with whiskers and a long tail sent her over the edge.

Peter was mystified. What was going on? What had happened to him the past few minutes?

"You didn't hear me?"

"I swear," Peter said.

Hannah nodded her head and circled the room. "Well, you know what that means, don't you?"

"I really don't."

Hannah put her arms around his neck. She felt warm against him. "This is where your studio's going to be."

"My…?"

"Are you okay? Earth to Peter."

"Sorry, I guess I went away there for a bit."

She hugged him closer. "That's all right. It's an odd day. First your dad, then this place. I'm just saying that if you couldn't hear me shouting my head off—and believe me, I was—then how great would it be to finally have a little nook where you can record without having to worry about your noisy wife."

Peter stepped away from her and took in the room. It had awful mint green walls and smelled like dirt. Faded crayon drawings were strewn about the floor—he was standing on one.

"I don't know."

"I'll help you paint it. Make it nice. We can take that plaid couch from your folks' place—you know, the hide-a-bed in the guest room—and put it along that wall. Maybe a little fridge for your iced teas? Hmm?"

Peter lifted his foot and looked down at the drawing. It was nothing but a white sheet of paper covered in a frantic scribble of black crayon. More clutter for the trash.

"Maybe."

"Down here, Peter, you wouldn't hear a peep."

The scream from upstairs contradicted her.

* * *

They found Lillian Dann in the living room.

"Oh, my God!" the realtor was shouting. "Oh, my!"

She stood cowering at the doorway, pointing toward the gaping maw of the brick fireplace. Soot and charcoaled bits littered the floor. And in the middle of the room flapped a black, screaming thing.

"Jesus," said Hannah. "Is that a bird?"

"It's a crow. It's a damn crow," cried Lillian. "I do *not* do birds, I swear to God."

Peter took a step toward the crow. It spotted him instantly and screeched a warning. It flapped its wings wildly, threatening to take to the air. He fell back, and the bird toppled to the floor.

"Where'd it come from?" Hannah asked.

"Down the chimney," Lillian said, looking for all the world as if she would bolt. "Filthy thing! I can't look, I can't look."

Hannah squatted down to get a better look at the bird, which was now hopping about, scattering ash in cryptic patterns on the floor. "What's wrong with it?"

"It's got a broken wing," Peter said.

It did at that. The crow's left wing was flopping at the joint, twisting back and forth. It reminded Peter of the way Hannah had taught him how to tuck back the wings of a turkey before roasting.

"Open the window," Lillian shouted at Peter. It was strange seeing this very put-together woman so unraveled.

"It can't fly out."

"Let's go. We can leave the doors open. Let's go!" The woman was near panic.

Hannah looked up at Peter. "We can't leave it, Peter."

She was right, of course. As always. But doing the right thing was going to be difficult. And messy.

He turned to Lillian Dann. "You go wait out front. I'll come find you when I'm done."

"Thank you, thank you," the realtor sputtered. She was gone in a shot.

Peter looked back to the crow. It stared, no…*glared* at him, daring him to move an inch closer.

"So, Mr. Larson, how are we going to do this?" Hannah had adopted her matter of fact tone, the one she used for all unpleasant tasks.

Peter took a quick inventory of the room and settled on the Mexican blanket balled up in the corner—wouldn't Lillian Dann have a field day with *that*. He stepped around the bird, which staggered forward, keeping its focus squarely on him.

He snagged the blanket and gave it a shake. Dust billowed. He grabbed two corners and held it out in front of him like a magician about to perform his next trick.

Watch me make this crow disappear.

"Back away," he said. Hannah rose slowly, but there had been no need. The bird's black eyes had locked on Peter's.

"Careful, Peter."

"Do me a favor. When I say *now*, I want to you to distract him."

"How do you want me to do that?"

"Flap your arms, whistle Dixie; I don't care. Just do it, okay, baby?"

"You got it."

The crow hissed.

Jesus Christ. They can hiss?

Peter took a step forward. "Okay, hush now. Hush."

The bird didn't hush. It spat and waved its distorted wing at him like a curse.

He took another step. He was almost within tossing distance of the bird.

"All right. One…two…"

"Are you counting or are you saying *now*?"

"Both, Hannah. One…two…"

The crow let loose a defiant crap.

"Three. Now!"

Hannah took a loud step toward the bird, waving her arms and singing at the top of her lungs. *"You're a grand old flag! You're a high-flying flag! And forever in peace may you wave!"*

The bird rose up, squawking and spitting. Turning its attention toward Hannah, it began leapfrogging her way.

Hannah retreated. "Peter!"

Peter made his move. He threw the blanket over the top of the crow, but it landed short. The bird wriggled free and turned back to face him.

"Shit!"

Peter dove for the blanket and raised it up like a catcher's mitt as the bird charged. He felt it strike, felt it squirm beneath his hands. He quickly swaddled the screaming thing, leaving no trace of it uncovered save for its angry, clacking beak.

He looked at Hannah. She was staring at him with wide-eyed wonder. "You got it."

"Damn straight."

"Now what?"

"Now you go keep Lillian company."

He rose, carefully holding the writhing bundle close, but not too close. The bird was anxious to take a bite out of anything it could.

"What are you going to do?"

"Please?" he begged. Hannah flashed him a sad smile and left the room.

The bird wriggled, and one of its clawed feet dug through the blanket and into his arm. Peter responded by shaking the bundle, dislodging the talons.

Out back. Take it out back.

Peter strode down the hallway toward the back door. When he reached it, he kicked it open. Its upper hinge broke loose—just another item to add to the fix-it list for this damn place.

The smell of harvest was thick in the air. The workers had taken a break for lunch, but the scent of freshly-picked soybeans still wafted in the late September air. It was sweet and powdery.

Near the edge of the pond sat a small, pile of stones. Bigger than skipping stones, they would do the trick. The crow seemed to sense his motives and resumed its pecking and clawing.

Get this done quick.

Peter kneeled. The ground was saturated with water, and he realized that the pond didn't have any firm edge, any clear line of delineation between land and water.

He clutched the bundle tight with his left hand while his right searched out a stone. He caught a glimpse of the ragged marks on his right forearm, and his thoughts returned to the basement. To the scratched door.

Skahhh!

The bird's anger was turning venomous—he could feel its strength rising beneath his grip.

His hand found the perfect stone, and he wasted no time. He raised it high over his head and brought it down hard.

The bird let out a *Kah!* But its squirming only increased. The problem was instantly clear—the ground was too soggy. With every blow, he'd only pound the crow's head deeper and deeper into the pliant soil.

Peter peered out over the pond. It was a beautiful day, it really was. Too beautiful to fill a Mexican blanket with rocks, tie it tight and toss it—crow, stones and all—into the water.

And yet, that's exactly what he did.

* * *

Lillian Dann and Hannah were waiting for him out front near the cars.

"How'd you make out?" Hannah asked.

"Fine," he said, hiding his trembling hands.

"I am *so* sorry, Peter," Lillian said. "I could never stomach a bird. Ask anyone. Still, that was very unprofessional of me, and I apologize, I apologize, I apologize."

Peter smiled. The woman seemed truly upset. "It's all right."

"I'm going to go," Lillian said as she hopped into her Mini. "Your wife gave me all your contact info—emails and whatnot. I'm going have a chitchat with the cleaning crew I use and see if we can't knock twenty percent off a good sweep of this place for you. Same with your folks' house. Get you settled on both fronts. I'll be in touch real, real soon, but right now, I've got to go."

And with that, the realtor steered her Mini down the drive, kicking up gravel as she went.

"Now *that's* a woman who doesn't like birds," Hannah said.

Peter didn't reply. His thoughts were on the bundle at the bottom of the pond.

"Was it bad?" Hannah asked.

"Yeah, it was."

She kissed him on the cheek. "It's one-two-three-*go*, by the way. Not one-two-three-*now*."

"Where the hell did you pull *You're a Grand Old Flag* from?"

Hannah smiled. "It worked, didn't it?"

Peter sighed and rolled his shoulders. He looked out over the brown front lawn and at the brown vista beyond.

"C'mon," his wife said, pulling him toward the car. "I think you need a little day drinkin'."

As they pulled away from the house, Peter could have sworn he heard it laughing.

CHAPTER 8

Peter ushered Hannah through the door of the Blind Rock Tavern, grateful for the cool comfort of the place.

"Blind Rock?" Hannah mused. "What's the story there?"

"Haven't a clue," Peter answered. He had spotted the place after their meeting with Moots and had tucked it into his mental Rolodex for later. "We'll have to ask."

The Blind Rock consisted of a single room that extended back into darkness almost half a block. A row of video poker machines lined the wall next to the restrooms, giving off the occasional electronic bleep.

The joint was empty, save for the bartender—a gangly fellow with a shock of dark hair and a goatee. The man looked up as they entered.

"What can I get you, folks?"

"Do you mind if we just sit a sec?" Peter asked.

The bartender waved them in. "No problem. You want some music?"

It was Hannah who answered. "Why not?"

"A little Willie coming up." The man ducked below the counter, and a second later, "On the Road Again" kicked in over the sound system. Peter and Hannah chose a booth and plunked down. Hannah drummed her fingers on the tabletop in time with the music. *On the road again...*

"You want a shot?" Peter asked.

"It's not even noon, Mr. Larson."

"Do you want one?"

"Yes, please."

Peter rose and headed for the bar. The bartender was busy loading Jägermeister into a three-bottle tap dispenser.

"Change your mind?" the man asked.

Peter eyed the bottles on the shelf. "What do you have in the way of whiskey?"

"Whiskey whiskey or bourbon whiskey?"

"Bourbon."

"Let's see. I've got Jim Beam, Knob Creek, Old Crow—"

"Nix on the Old Crow," Peter said. "Tell me, what's the worst bourbon you've got?"

"The worst?"

"Seriously, the very worst. Rotgut through and through."

The bartender raised a plastic bottle filled with a pale brown liquid. "Ballen's. Now *that's* the worst. It used to be our house bourbon, but no one could stomach it."

"Then why do you keep it around?"

The barkeep grinned. "Why, for moments like this, of course. An extra buck and I'll make it a beer and a bump."

"A beer and a—?"

"Coors and a shot. Takes the edge off."

"Why not. Two, please."

"It's Riggs."

Peter squinted at the man. "Oh. Peter."

"I'll bring 'em right over."

Peter sauntered back to the booth.

"I like this," Hannah said.

"What?"

"Being here in the dark in the middle of the day. I like the stupid little Christmas lights over the bar that you know they never take down. It reminds me of undergrad."

"Spent a lot of time in dives like this, did we?"

"Hell no!" Hannah retorted. "This is a hundred times classier. There was this one joint I bartended back in Newark, the Rusty Nail, now *that* was a dive. This one time, this hooker who worked out of the men's room—"

Peter stopped her. "Is this a true story or a fake story?"

Hannah punched him in the arm. "Why do you do that? You know I like my stories."

"I just wanted to know if it was true."

"No! But that doesn't mean that I didn't bartend."

Peter squeezed her knee. "Okay, go ahead."

"No, you had your chance. That story's gone forever."

"C'mon."

"Nope."

Peter rubbed his hands. Hannah responded by rubbing hers in imitation.

"So," she said. "Are we taking the house or what?"

The bartender arrived carrying two red solo cups of beer and two shots of whiskey.

"Sorry about the wait," the man said, setting their beer on the table. "And for the plastic cups. Our dishwasher's gone tits up. But what's that they say?" Suddenly, he burst into song. "Red solo cup, I fill you up. Let's have a party!"

Hannah and Peter stared at each other a moment and then burst out laughing.

"What the…?" Hannah asked between giggles.

"You know? The Toby Keith tune?"

Peter shook his head. "I'm sorry…Riggs, was it? I haven't kept up on country top twenty."

The bartender set down the drinks and scowled. "What kind of crack is that, you piece of shit?"

Both Peter and Hannah froze.

"No crack," said Peter, shifting nervously. "I didn't mean anything by it. Honest."

"Yeah?"

"Honest."

The man slapped him on the shoulder. "For God's sake, Pete. It's Riggs."

Peter was at a loss for words. One of the video poker games let loose an electronic chirp. And then it dawned on him.

"Riggs?"

"And the penny drops!"

Peter grabbed the guy's hand, and Riggs immediately pulled him in for a bear hug. "God, what the hell happened to your hair? You look like Einstein fucked Jerry Garcia."

"Damn, tell me what you really think."

Peter turned to his wife. "Hannah, this is Eli Riggs. We went to high school together."

Hannah, who had held her breath for the last minute, exhaled a great *ahhh!*

"Good ole MCS. Of course, I was a lowly freshman and he was a seniorino."

"We also worked a summer together at the county pool."

"That's right, the pool!" Riggs cried. "All that pee!"

Riggs leaned over Hannah. "What did you ever do in life to deserve a bozo like this?"

"I lost a bet."

Riggs chortled. "Ho! She's a good one. You're a good one. Lemme grab a brewski and join you." He leaped up and practically ran back to the bar. "You two in town long?"

"For awhile. Is this your place?" Peter asked.

Riggs grabbed a cup from the stack, flipped it in the air and caught it coolly. "Naw, this is just my part-time, mostly full-time gig. I manage the joint. Summer's are easy. But come fall things are going to get downright ugly."

"Why's that?" Hannah asked.

Riggs returned with his beer and hovered over the table. "The college kids. As soon as they step foot in town, they'll be right back here. And I just lost my best drink slinger. Love the shirt, by the way, Hannah."

"Thanks."

"Mighty fuckin' sweet. You want me to play some Leppard?"

"No thanks."

"Yeah, it may not look like it right now, but the old Rock can rake in the dough."

Peter glanced around the room. Now that he thought about it, there was something about the place that looked familiar. "This wasn't always here."

"Ding-ding-ding!" Riggs sat with a plop. "Used to be Pizza Carl's, but they shut that shithole down years ago. Rats in the garbage disposal. Hey, at least they were trying to get rid of them, know what I mean?" He raised his cup. "Here's to rattlesnakes and condoms—two things I never screw with." Hannah snorted. Soon, all three of them were laughing.

"So, Pete," Riggs said. "You know how glowing my future turned out to be. What line of work did you end up in?"

"I'm a narrator."

"What, like on the Discovery Channel?"

"Nope, never had the knack for that. I record audiobooks." He already knew what was coming next. It was almost too easy to predict.

"Really? That's amazing. I check out tons from the library. Most self-help stuff. Tony Robbins and such. Always thought I'd like to try that. Maybe you'll give me some pointers?"

There it was.

"Sure."

Riggs turned to Hannah. "And how about you, sweetness? You making any babies for my buddy, here?"

Hannah went pale.

Riggs instantly realized his mistake. "Oh, Jeez. Did I—?"

Hannah forced a smile and put her hand on his arm. "It's okay. Will you excuse me?"

Peter started to rise. "Hannah?"

"It's okay. You two boys catch up. I've got to pee."

She extricated herself from the booth and dashed past the scolding poker machines, escaping into the women's room.

"Aw, man," Riggs sighed. "I put my foot in it, didn't I? I'm always doing shit like that. My ex used to say that if there was a pile of crap within a hundred square miles, my fucking foot would find it."

Peter got up. "I'm going to go check on her."

"Yeah, of course."

Peter headed for the restrooms, leaving Riggs surrounded by plastic cups and shot glasses. "And *that's* why I drink alone."

* * *

Peter found Hannah leaning against a graffiti-covered wall.

"I miss him," she said. "I miss my Michael."

"I know."

"I miss him *so* much!"

He held her close as her sobs shook them both. And he made the decision for her. They were moving into the house—the house of the broken bird. They were moving in and fixing everything. The house, themselves, the whole goddamn world.

CHAPTER 9

They made love as soon as they got back to the motel. It was wild and necessary. Neither of them even had the chance to undress fully. And when it was over, they attacked the pizza Riggs had sent them home with by way of an apology.

Home.

At that moment it meant the Intermission Motor Lodge, and that was okay.

The clock radio told Peter that it was 3:30 in the afternoon, that there were hours left to hide away in before the dawn of their new lives. And so, hide away they would.

Hannah stole the last piece of pizza out from under his nose. "Mine!" she grinned. He let her have it.

She grabbed two remotes from the nightstand—one for the ceiling fan, the other for the TV—and set the fan on high and the TV on HBO. She pulled the comforter up around herself, leaving him the sheets, and ate her pizza.

"Comfy?"

"Very," she said. "Very very."

"Good."

Hannah stopped at the crust. She never ate her crusts. "Do you remember what his favorite pizza was?"

"Mushroom, all the way."

"That's right."

"Just like his dad."

"Disgusting." Hannah curled up her nose. "You two *loved* the fact that I can't stand them. He'd always sneak one onto one of my slices. Oh, and was he crafty? Sometimes he'd sneak it under the cheese."

"That's my boy."

They both paused at his use of the present tense, letting it hang in the air between them.

"He would've liked this," Hannah said as she dropped the ceiling fan down to medium. "He always loved a motel."

"Swimming."

"The ice machine."

"Finding the Bible in the nightstand drawer."

"Or the Book of Mormon. Remember that?" Hannah smiled. "What a can of worms *that* opened."

"Where was that? Iowa?"

"Nauvoo. Remember? It was the day your dad took us all down to Keokuk to look for geodes, and a hot air balloon suddenly appeared in the sky, floating over the Mississippi? Remember?"

"I remember," Peter said, but the memory was foggy. That day, like so many others he'd spent with Michael, was already slipping away. Like a dream.

Hannah reached out for his hand.

"You've got sauce on your fingers," Peter protested.

"Take it, you big dope."

He did.

"We did the best we could, right?"

"One hundred percent right."

"He didn't want for anything."

"Not a thing."

"We did our job. And now it's time to move on. Right?"

"That's right, sweetheart."

She sat back, content to leave it there. But Peter wasn't finished. If they were talking, they were talking.

"You'll never try to hurt yourself again, right?" He had said the words to her a hundred times in his head since that day—since Hannah's Bad Day—but hearing them aloud felt like stepping to the edge of a cliff, not knowing if he'd fall or not.

Hannah offered him her open face, and the sorrow and shame Peter found there broke his heart.

"Right," she said. She crawled over, took his chin between her thumb and forefinger and kissed him.

* * *

Peter rose in the middle of the night and slipped into the bathroom, careful not to turn on the light lest he wake Hannah.

He hadn't slept a wink. He had watched as the clock doled out the hours like a miser and now, at 4:02 in the morning, he had given up any hope of falling asleep.

It wasn't the bed—it was comfortable enough. Nor was it Hannah's night prattle. She had always mumbled in her sleep, and it had never kept him up. He found it comforting, in fact, to listen to her dreamy commentary—a reassurance in the night that she was there.

What stole his slumber was the clicking of the ceiling fan as it spun round and round. He had tried to fish the remote out from under Hannah's arm, but every time he tried, she'd stir. The last thing he wanted was to rob her of her sleep.

He rose and tiptoed to the bathroom. He flipped the light switch, and blue-whiteness filled the room, illuminating a framed poster of an old Maple City Fall Festival poster, circa 1974. Rides, games, a tractor pull and a haystack scramble for the kids. *This year's Fall Festival Queen: Shelly Harding!* A photo of Shelly sat in the corner of the poster, wearing her tiara and waving. *Probably the best day of her entire life,* Peter thought.

He held his arm out over the sink and examined the claw marks the ruthless crow had gifted him. Not too deep, but red and angry. Three parallel scrapes. Like exclamation marks without the dots.

Hannah has the dots.

And suddenly, Hannah's Bad Day came lumbering into the room, elbowing its way into his consciousness before he could fend it off. He gripped the edge of the sink.

Hannah's Bad Day, a flip term his mind had come up with to lessen the blow of what he had seen that afternoon in their apartment. He had just completed recording the first book in the *Benjamin Coffin* series at the Flatiron studios. It was a Tuesday night, and the Larsons had always been true to Taco Tuesday. Jesús' Taqueria made Hannah's favorites, and so he had swung by on his way home, bringing a hulking bagful of soft shell tacos and all the fixings.

Nothing seemed amiss when he had dumped the food in the kitchen, nor when he hung up his bike and quickly checked his email. But when Hannah hadn't answered, when he saw that the YouTube clip of Michael's third birthday at

Liberty State Park was frozen on the TV screen, Peter's heart had grown loud in his chest.

He'd made a beeline for Michael's room, and found his wife sitting up against the wall next to the radiator where the hospital bed once stood. She'd had an old IV line in her hand, its needled point dripping red, her other arm peppered with nasty self-inflicted wounds, weeping blood.

"You'll never try to hurt yourself again, right?"

Peter opened a small courtesy soap, lathered up his arm. The scent of lilac filled the air. Michael always hated lilac.

He stole a moment to look at himself in the mirror before heading to bed. The face he saw was tired and burdened. He'd have to change that. But not tonight.

After peeing and flushing the toilet ever so slowly, ever so quietly, he returned to the bed. Hannah still defended the remote.

"More than it was going to be…" she said to no one.

And so Peter endured the offending fan. *Click, click, click.* Over and over again. In time, the sound became the clicking of a bird's beak—open, closed, open, closed—bringing visions of broken wings, squirming bundles and bubbles on the surface of the water.

CHAPTER 10

The crayon snapped in the boy's hand. He took a huge intake of breath, filling his lungs to the point of bursting.

Awake!

He was alone in the room. The thing—the nightmare thing—was gone.

The boy could feel his heart racing like a rabbit in his chest, feel the uncomfortable dampness in his pajama bottoms. He was miserable, but he was *awake.*

He looked down at the drawings scattered in front of him on the floor. Stick figures danced on each in violent tangos, seemingly in another's hand as he had graduated from stick figures years ago.

The most recent lay before him in all its bloody splendor. A grey, crooked man curled around a cowered woman, and there was blood in his teeth. The eyes of both figures were wild, crazed—his in anger, hers in unhinged fear.

The man's fingers dug into the woman's head. This is where the majority of the red crayon, the crayon he had snapped, was used.

A scrawled caption accompanied the tableau.

BAD

As he stared at the drawing, it began to move. The stick man circling the stick woman, much like the thing from his nightmare circled his room. The man gnashed his scribbled teeth while the woman fled, weeping waxy tears.

The man pursued. *BAD.* His mouth moving closer. *BAD.* Teeth bared. *BAD.* Biting down. *DAD.* Ripping her apart.

The boy grabbed the first crayon he could find—the black, *YES*, the black—and attacked the drawing, murdering the image, blotting it from view.

His hand circled like an incantation. The figures beneath raced, trying to avoid his scrawl, but they were no match for the boy's fevered efforts.

Soon, the page was filled with black, the crayon worn down to a nub. Colors beneath tried to claw their way out, but the boy's mark was too strong. The red faded, bowing to the black, and the drawing ceased its restless movement.

The boy tossed aside his used-up crayon. He rose and ran for the doorway, passing through it and into the darkness, heading for the stairs beyond.

CHAPTER 11

The man at the Ryder truck lot was none too pleased when Peter called to inform him that they'd need the truck for a couple more days.

"How many?" the guy on the other end of the line grumbled.

"Two, maybe three," Peter said.

"You just pissed all over my shoes, mister," the man said and hung up.

Hannah reached out to Lillian Dann about getting someone in to give the place a good clean before they started moving their prized possessions and learned that her preferred cleaning company consisted of her son, her nephews and a family friend.

"I am *so* glad this is going to work out for you!" she crooned. "I'll have my Tad round up his gang. They're family, so they're good." She lowered her voice. "Except for Juan, of course. Not that he's not *good*, but…you know. He's just not family."

The team met them at the house at eight the next morning, armed with cleaning supplies and contractor bags.

"Where do want us to start?" asked Juan. He apparently did the speaking for the group.

Peter, who had always felt odd about hiring people to do his work for him, pointed in the general direction of the house. "Wherever you want."

Juan rounded up the crew, and they headed into the house, like troops ready to do battle. The team went to town on the place, hauling out mattresses, broken furniture and, to everyone's amusement, a plastic kiddie pool someone had left upstairs to chill their brewskis.

"You mind if I have this?" Juan asked Peter. "Not a crack in it."

"It's yours," Peter said.

Around noon, Hannah flagged him down.

"I'm going into town," she said. She was wearing her grey slacks and red top. She meant business.

"Oh, yeah?"

"Yup. I'm gonna see what kind of jobs this ole town of yours has to offer."

"Door to door? That's old school. Got your resume?"

"Of course, dear."

"And your phone?"

"Don't get smart, dear." Hannah was notorious for leaving her phone behind.

"Then, get outta here. Looks like we're going to be cranking for the rest of the day."

Hannah looked back at the workers. The majority lazed about in the front yard, sipping Cokes or munching on sandwiches. Juan and a young girl were still inside, kicking up dust.

Hannah offered him her cheek. "Wish me luck, husband."

Peter kissed her, careful not to muss her clothes. "Go get 'em, tiger."

She strutted off toward the Prius, and he could tell she was feeling good about herself. A moment later, she had disappeared down the drive.

Peter turned back to the work at hand. "Who wants to clean out a kitchen?"

* * *

As Hannah drove the streets of Peter's youth—through neighborhoods foreign to her—she found it strange not having her husband by her side. The houses she passed seemed to whisper at her arrival. *Newcomer.*

The Prius hiccupped, reminding her that an oil change was probably in order.

She came to the town square and circled the statue of a city forefather standing watch, following the signs toward the college.

Hannah couldn't imagine growing up in a small town. She had always been a suburban gal, and later, an urban gal. The wide open spaces didn't quite make her uneasy but damn close to it. She'd get used to it; she was sure of that. But the idea of a town with one grocery store, one hospital, one Chinese restaurant was still a lot to absorb.

After picking her way through town to the campus, she pulled past the main Maple City College sign and steered down a serpentine road toward a cluster of administration buildings perched on a rise. Cue *Pomp and Circumstance,* she mused.

There was no space left in the visitor parking, and so she nosed into a space in the student parking lot. She grabbed her legal pad and scribbled *Visitor* in Sharpie and set it on the dash.

As she walked to the building, all the smells of autumn hit her at once, and they put a spring in her step.

* * *

At 2:30, Juan pulled Peter aside. "I think you're good. We finished upstairs and downstairs. I can send my cousin back later with a weed whacker and mower. Only place left is the basement. You want us to do the basement?"

Peter hesitated. Of course, he wanted them to clear out the basement, *needed* them to, but he felt a small twinge of possessiveness when he thought of Lillian's crew tromping around downstairs amongst the junk his father had left there. Perhaps it was a project he wanted to tackle himself.

"Did Lillian mention the house over on Oak?"

"Yeah," said Tad, Lillian's gawkishly tall son. "She said maybe we'd get to that tomorrow?" There was a hopeful tone in his voice.

"I'd love for you to head over there now if you don't mind. I want you to give it a good airing out. No need to box anything up just yet. There's a key under the frog on the front porch."

There were unspoken grumbles from the crew as they headed for their trucks.

"Juan," Peter called. "Any chance you could stay behind?"

The man looked to Tad. "Sure, but he's my ride."

"I'll get you home. I just need an extra back."

"You got it."

Peter waved him over to the Ryder truck and lifted the roll-up door. His planning had paid off—his audio booth was right up front.

"Howdy, partner," he said.

* * *

The director of human resources was an affable woman, but Hannah could tell quite soon that a job at the college wasn't in the cards. She looked Hannah's resume up and down before passing it back to her and offering up her most sympathetic smile.

"All of our positions are posted on the HR webpage," the woman in the powder blue suit explained. "Delia puts the new ones up as soon as we get them. Some from maintenance, adjunct positions, cafeteria staff, but mostly admin stuff, like you're looking for. Unfortunately, I haven't had a job for her to post in, I'd say, two months. Lord knows, we've always been on the quiet side when it comes to hiring, but this year we're positively silent."

The woman had refused her resume, insisting that she visit the webpage.

She was met with similar responses at the public library, the local paper and city hall.

"I think you're overqualified."

"We actually just laid off a couple of folks."

"Have you tried the college?"

72

And so, when she spotted the Coors Lite sign in the window of the Blind Rock Tavern as she was driving down Main Street, Hannah flipped the turn signal and headed for the adjacent municipal lot.

* * *

"That does it," Peter said as Juan maneuvered the final sectional wall into place. The worker had done him the service of replacing all the light bulbs in the basement from a box conveniently labeled *Light bulbs*. The two of them had managed to transport the booth piece by piece down to the small, basement room and were putting in the final screws that held the thing in place.

"You get inside?" Juan asked.

"That's right."

"And read the book?"

"That's about the size of it."

Juan looked rather impressed. "And they pay you?"

"Strange world, huh?"

Juan pondered this. "That's good. That's a good job."

"I suppose so. Thanks for hanging back to help me. I would never have gotten this down here myself." He fished around in his pocket for a twenty, then realized that he had given the last of his cash to Hannah. He stuck his other hand in his pocket as well, trying to disguise his thwarted tip. "Let's get out of here."

They sidestepped the plastic crates containing Peter's recording equipment—mic stand, preamp, coils of audio cable—and headed for the stairs.

Juan stopped dead in his tracks.

"Juan?" Peter asked. "Something wrong?"

The man seemed rooted to the spot.

"Juan?"

Tears started rolling down Juan's face.

"What's wrong?"

Juan looked perplexed. "I don't know. I don't know why I'm…" Wave after wave of tears poured down his cheeks.

Peter clapped him on the arm. "C'mon, let's get you some air."

The other man broke free and rushed to the stairs, bounding up them, making the whole staircase shake.

* * *

Riggs perused Hannah's resume a moment before tearing it up and tossing the scraps into the trash. He held out his hand.

"When can you start?"

"You don't even know if I know a muddler from a mop," she said.

"Mop gets a lot more action around here than the muddler, but if you wanna strut your stuff, how's about you make me a Rum Martinez?"

Hannah slipped behind the bar, removing her coat. "You want that with or without the applewood smoke?"

"Surprise me."

She grabbed a bottle of dark rum and got down to business.

"I'm sorry about that crack I made yesterday," Riggs said. "I was way outta line. I hope you'll let me make it up to you."

Hannah flipped a maraschino cherry into the air and caught it in the mixing glass. "Giving me a job would be a great start."

* * *

Back upstairs, Peter found Juan standing in the front yard, his arms folded and his head down.

"I'm sorry," he said, his eyes on the ground. "Please don't tell Mrs. Dann."

"Don't worry about it."

"I need this job."

"It's nothing, Juan. Are you okay?"

A distant train whistle echoed across the plains. "Can you drive me home?" Juan asked.

"Let me get my keys." Peter headed for the house. He paused next to the plastic swimming pool. "Can't let you forget this."

Juan didn't respond, and when they drove off down the road, the pool was still sitting in the front yard.

* * *

The sun was setting by the time Peter returned with the truck. Juan hadn't said a word during the drive. When Peter had pulled up to Juan's house, the man jumped out of the truck before it came to a full stop.

As he pulled up next to the house, he saw that the Prius was back. Next to it sat parked a Midwest Connections van. The internet serviceman that he'd scheduled for earlier this morning. Some things never changed.

"Hannah?" Peter called as he stepped inside.

"Back here!" she replied. "Near the back door."

He found her and the handsome service tech in the room at the rear of the house where the door to the basement stood open.

"This is Lance. He says this is the best spot to make sure the whole house is covered. Especially your booth." Hannah made it a habit of finding out workmen's first names.

"All up and running," Lance said. He turned to Hannah and handed her his card. "That's my cell in case you have any problems."

The serviceman had Hannah sign off on the work and took his leave. Peter fished the card out of Hannah's hand.

"Lance, eh?" he said, his voice dripping with insinuation.

"Stop."

"He gave you his digits, hmm?"

She gave him a shove. "The place looks great. How'd you make out with the crew?"

Juan's face popped into his head, and he closed the door. "Fine. My booth's already downstairs. I'll get up early and upload some audio samples, which I can now do thanks to *Lance.*"

Hannah wrinkled her nose at him. The jealousy game was fun, but only in small doses.

"And you?" Peter asked.

"You're looking at the Blind Rock's newest bartender, my friend."

"OMG. You're kidding me. When do you start?"

"Saturday. I told your buddy that my husband needed my help unpacking tomorrow. So, what do you think?"

"I think you're amazing."

Hannah walked over to Peter and put her arms around his neck. She kissed him gently. "Now, can you go get the Aerobed out of the truck, Mr. Larson? I think I'm in desperate need of a cuddle."

"Anything you want, Mrs. Larson."

CHAPTER 12

At first, Peter didn't know where he was. As his eyes adjusted, he recognized the lines of the room where he had found Hannah the night before, laid out in the inflatable bed beneath the poster of New York City she'd hung above it. A regular Mary Bailey waiting for her George.

For the second night in a row, his sleep had been fitful, sparse and the shreds of relief he'd managed to piece together didn't add up to a full night's rest.

He lay next to Hannah on the inflatable bed, listening to the house creak. The room Hannah had settled on for their master bedroom was rather sizable with a row of windows looking out over the backyard, over the pond. The wallpaper was pale and faded, and it would need to come down.

There was something odd about the house, that much he knew, but he was determined not to let his mind run wild. True, he had had his initial jitters in the basement, and there were Juan's tears. But odd wasn't terrible and it sure as hell wasn't a deal-breaker. Besides, there were countless other times he had gotten a sense of something being off. In neighborhoods where he had quickened his pace, in certain taxis he had taken. In Michael's empty bedroom before Hannah's deep dive. And weren't those times more reflections of himself than his location?

Sheesh! Enough with the philosophy, Professor.

He forced himself to get up. He slipped on his sweatpants from the night before—the ones Hannah had so eagerly stolen from him—and searched around for his shoes.

Flipping on the overhead lights, he descended the stairs to the first floor and tried to see the place as he imagined Hannah saw it. New coats of paint, a throw rug or two. Potted ferns. Did she like potted ferns?

He reached the foyer and double-checked that the front door was locked—it was. As he passed the stairs and headed down the hall past the living room, he realized that he'd have to write Larson Enterprises a check for one dollar tomorrow. Strange days indeed.

The door to the basement was open.

"I'll have to put a latch on you," Peter said to the open door, keeping his nerves in check.

He flipped the switch, and the basement lit up.

Time to make the donuts.

* * *

By the time Peter had pieced his recording equipment back into its familiar configuration, snaking cords from his laptop to the preamp and into the booth, he was eager to get to work. Once he had placed his ergonomic chair inside and rigged up his fancy German microphone, Peter stepped inside and checked it out.

It was the same booth he'd been using for years, bought off Craigslist from a musician in Brooklyn. When asked why there was a latch at the top of the door—allowing it to be locked from the outside—the man replied, "My kid just turned three, and equipment's expensive."

Through the vertical window in the door, he could peer at the room outside, but other than that, the effect was much like being tucked away inside an oversized phone booth. Or a padded cell.

Having positioned the booth inside this little room, the recording environment felt doubly soundproofed. No more waiting for planes to pass overhead, no more two-hour pauses waiting for the neighbors to finish washing and drying their sneakers. *Thunk-thunk-thunk.*

He sat and adjusted the height of the chair. Perfect. This was going to work just fine. He switched on the power to his system and made a little prayer. *Please, don't trip the breaker.* The little lights on the preamp flickered on. All was good.

Peter powered up his tablet and found the Wi-Fi signal. Hannah had named the network *homesweethome.* Soon, he was searching through the folder he shared with the team at Flatiron Audio. He opened the folder labeled *p_larson.*

"Thank you, thank you," he sighed. There was a long list of pdfs, each with accompanying titles such as *The Birthday Doctor* and *Squirrel's Holiday.* Instead of the usual dozen or so titles the company assigned narrators working a thirteen-week contract, Mika and the good folks at Flatiron Audio had filled his queue with children's books. Minimal prep time, funny voices, zero need for his dictionary of geographical place names.

"One of today's wins," Peter whispered, echoing a daily tally he and Hannah had started back when Michael had first gotten sick. The big stuff was overwhelming—why not celebrate the little victories? Drinking an especially good cup of coffee, finding a MetroCard with twenty dollars on it, catching a pocketed pen before it made it into the laundry. Little victories. Today's wins. Finger holds on the cliff of life.

He opened the first title, *Iggy Ostrich*, and scanned the text. After settling on a passage to record, Peter put on his headphones, opened the Vocable recording program and proceeded to set his levels. He recorded the section a number of times, making adjustments as he went.

Finally, he was ready to record the first take.

"This is Peter Larson testing studio levels for Flatiron Audio. I'll be reading from *Iggy Ostrich* by Ronald Orson Platt."

CHAPTER 13

The boy ran through the basement, hands out in front of him, ready to fend off whatever he might encounter.

He made a beeline for the stairs, the lone overhead bulb a beacon. But as he ran, his vision tightened. The staircase receded into the distance, growing smaller like an image seen through a pinhole camera. It shrank, threatening to blink out of existence entirely.

Suddenly, the stairs veered to his left, and he was certain he would throw up. Nausea welled up inside him the likes of which he hadn't felt since the Old Man had spun him wildly about on the merry-go-round at the park, laughing at his pleas to stop, reveling in his screams. Now, as then, he felt like he was going to fall off the end of the world.

"Stop!" he cried.

Cold breath played across the back of his neck, and something snickered, "Stop!"

The staircase shifted again, to the right and behind him. He whirled about slowly as if underwater, fighting against the tide. He got the stairs in his sights and pressed on.

Stick figures raged in his head, fighting, cavorting, doing things his seven-year-old mind could not comprehend. Crayon hands dug into his brain. There was laughter, too— inside and out—pounding behind his eyes, bouncing against the walls. He tried to scream, but a waxy film filled his mouth.

"You can't scribble me out!" he cried, spitting crayon shavings as he ran.

Without warning, the staircase rose up before him, and he ran headlong into it, striking his shinbones on the bottommost step with a *crack*. He tumbled face-first onto the stairs. Wasting no time, for surely the thing was behind him ready to pounce, the boy scrambled upward.

The steps behind him groaned under the weight of something large, something heavy, but he didn't look back. He crawled frantically until he finally reached the door.

The boy grabbed the doorknob and twisted.

Locked!

Laughter behind him—low and guttural—like water gurgling down a drain.

He pounded on the door and screamed.

"Daddy!"

CHAPTER 14

The waveform on the screen had flatlined.

Peter punched a key, and the timeline stopped. He scrolled the cursor back, watching the seconds of silence turn into minutes. One, two, three—hadn't he hit record?

Finally, he reached the jagged up and down of his recorded voice and clicked on the final few seconds.

"Never had Iggy had such a day!" the voice in his headphones chortled.

He rewound the remainder of the track and listened. Good stuff. Clear diction, delineated characters, a richness that the German mic brought to the table.

Puzzled, he quickly scrolled across the timeline and snipped out the three minutes of dead air. He'd zoned out before in the booth but usually only after a four or five-hour stint reading a diet book.

Happy with the take, he compressed the track, saving it in Flatiron's preferred format, and uploaded it to the *p_larson* folder.

Step one complete—he'd recorded his sample. Tomorrow, he'd get word of any adjustments the company might want, but he was more than certain there would be none. With over two hundred audiobooks recorded—most of them of the ten to twelve-hour variety—his ear was a pretty good judge when it came to levels. He recorded the sample and sent it off. Another of today's wins.

He shut down the system and stepped out of the booth into the little room. The basement was as quiet as…

He caught himself before allowing himself to touch on the word *grave*.

Peter headed back upstairs and snuggled in close to Hannah who was busy with her night chatter.

"Not that tooth…" she murmured.

"Okay," he said in a calm, low voice—his narrator's voice. "Not that tooth."

* * *

Breakfast consisted of egg sandwiches and a quart of orange juice Peter had picked up at a quick mart on the edge of town. The short ride there and back gave him a chance to catch up on the local AM radio. Farm reports, high school football scores and ads for the upcoming Fall Festival—there was a comfort in it that he couldn't quite describe.

They ate on the front porch, taking in the view. The sun was making its lazy ascent as a jet divided the sky with its contrails.

Peter eyed the Ryder truck. "I bet we can get it unloaded by noon."

"I bet we can get it unloaded by…eleven thirty-five," Hannah countered.

"I bet we can get it unloaded by—"

"Eleven twelve!" she said, stealing his thunder.

They were done before ten.

"Sometimes I forget how little we actually own," Hannah said as they carried in the last of the boxes.

"You forget the Great Purge of 2015 after I read that book about ridding your life of unnecessary baggage. Even Michael got in on the act."

Hannah smiled. "Poor guy tossed out his stuffed snake and then cried for days after wanting it back."

They caught each other's eye. They were testing new waters, touching these old memories. The message Peter got from Hannah was so far so good.

"I want to swing by my folks' place and check in on the crew," he said, setting down a box labeled *H's Many, Many Shoes.* "I also thought that, since I've got the truck, I'd pick up Dad's chair and take it over to his room."

"I don't hear a lot of *we* in that plan," Hannah said. "You want to go solo or can a lady hitch a ride?"

"How about if I head over first, get the chair, see Pop and meet you at the rental place. Maybe we could grab some lunch, check out the hardware store? I need to pick up a cordless drill."

"How could a girl say no?"

He left her unpacking her shoes and boots, pausing now and then to examine a favorite pair.

"I'll text you when I'm done."

"Mm-hmm," she said, admiring a pair of sleek, red cowboy boots she'd uncovered.

* * *

Tad and his team were hard at it by the time he pulled up in front of his parents' house with the truck. A row of garbage bags lined the curb. Peter soon learned that Juan had not shown up for work.

"Dude called in sick, can you believe it?" Tad said. "It's like he knew what was waiting for him in that kitchen. Pardon me saying so, but that was nasty."

"Sorry about that," Peter said. "Can one of you guys help me get the recliner into the truck?"

After hoisting the patched, leather chair into the payload, Peter thanked Tad and the crew, promising that he'd swing back by with some burgers and fries.

"Kinda lost my appetite, if you know what I mean," Tad said.

A fender bender at the end of the street diverted Peter's route through a more collegiate section of the neighborhood. Here rows of sorority and frat houses stood, the Greek letters seeming to go on forever. Would his childhood home become the next Sigma Chi house? How would Myrna Larson react if she found out?

"She'd probably start screaming at the bed," he said. His take on his mother had turned darkly humorous since her decline. But hey, whatever got you through.

No doubt he'd be hearing again soon from Lillian Dann and Mr. Moots. If the college was hot on snapping up the old homestead, one less thing on his plate. At least he could keep the government off their backs. And Applegate was decent enough. *They lay out a buffet on Sunday that's top notch,* Moots had said. Pop had always loved a Sunday buffet.

Upon arriving at the home, Peter had to decide between the handcart and the dolly to transport the chair. He chose the handcart and halfway to the front doors wished he had chosen the dolly. The chair wobbled treacherously as he pushed it, almost running a poor woman waiting for her ride off the sidewalk.

"Sorry!" he called, jabbing at the button for admittance. The woman merely glared at him.

As he wheeled the chair down the hall, he thought he felt envious eyes watching the recliner pass. It was a comfortable chair. His father had picked it at Goods Furniture years ago and had kept it patched and reclining, much to his mother's chagrin. Peter realized that its intrusion into her new living space might cause some friction, but frankly, he didn't care. He couldn't give Pop much, but he could give him his chair.

"He's at PT, and she's…I'm not sure where she is," said the nurse on duty. She eyed the chair like it was an unwelcome guest. "You really bringing that thing in here?"

Peter removed the uncomfortable, wooden chair from next to his father's bed and positioned the recliner so it had a good view of the window. He stepped back and viewed his work. Big Bear's throne. Maybe it was best if it just appeared in the room. Like magic.

When he got back to the truck, he called Gina. "I've got a crew cleaning up the house on Oak. Is there anything you want me to put aside for you?"

His sister sounded like she was in the middle of a dozen tasks, as always. "Photos, jewelry and Mom's doilies. Look, can I call you back later?"

A text alert chimed in his ear. "No problem," he told her. "I gotta take this anyway."

He looked down at the message.

Little tech issue. Call me.

It was from Mika at Flatiron.

She answered on the first ring. "Hey, Peter. No big deal. Your levels are fine. I just need you to do a double-check for glitches. You just about blew my engineer's ears out."

"Glitches?"

"Check the end of your file. Again, no redo—just send clean audio."

Peter apologized and assured her that he would.

He dialed Hannah as he headed for the Ryder truck office.

"I'm on my way to drop off the truck."

"Ooo, does that mean lunch?"

"Going to have to take a rain check. I need to check out the sample I sent."

"Nuts," Hannah said. "I was looking forward to trying my first tenderloin."

"Don't get hangry. Give me one hour in the booth, and I'll get you some strawberry-rhubarb pie. I'm sending you the rental place's address right now."

* * *

After returning the truck, Hannah dropped Peter back at the house.

"I need a couple of new outfits for work, and before you tell me I've got plenty to wear, let me remind you that I've still got those Visa gift cards my family gave me for my birthday. So there."

"There's not a big selection in town," Peter said. "What kinda look are you going for, Mrs. Larson?"

"I think yee-haw would best describe it."

"This I gotta see," Peter said. He gave her the directions to Bourne Farm Outfitters and sent her on her way with a slap on the butt. "Ride 'em, cowgirl."

Back in his booth, Peter loaded the *Iggy Ostrich* file. He visually scanned the file for the telltale sign of an ear-splitting glitch. He finally found the defective section and selected it.

Turning down the volume on his headphones, he hit play.

The sound that raged in his ear was like nails screaming down a chalkboard—an explosion of static and hiss. How in hell hadn't he caught it before turning in the sample?

He started to delete the section, caused by a bad cable connection no doubt, but stopped. He moved his cursor to the filters menu and viewed the selections: remove noise, high pass filter, anti-distortion. With each click of his mouse, the jagged waveform shrank. And after applying the seventh filter, he hit play once more.

A wind tunnel roar filled his ears, and a single word fought its way through the cacophony to reach him. When it did, it was enough to make Peter's heart seize in his chest.

"Daddy!"

Peter jolted as if he'd stepped on the third rail. He replayed the clip.

"Daddy!"

Sweat forming on his brow, he clicked a button, causing the section to loop.

"Daddy! Daddy! Daddy!"

He strained, trying to identify the voice, but it was evading him. All he could tell was that the speaker was young. And scared.

"Daddy! Daddy! Daddy!"

The repetition beat in his head like a chant, like a prayer. He raised the volume.

"Daddy! Daddy! DADDY!"

He felt fabric rustle against his face. He tried to resist. It reached up over his head, engulfing him. Cloth pressed down on his mouth, stifling him.

"Daddy?"

He raised his hand and fought against it, trying to break free of the invisible shroud that was hell-bent on stealing his breath.

"Daddy, stop it."

Peter struggled—against the haze he was falling into, against the voice, against...

"Stop it!"

Small hands pulled the sheet from his head.

"That's not funny anymore," Michael said.

Peter stared in disbelief. Sitting before him, propped up by pillows, was his son. He had a stern look on his face and not a single hair upon his smooth head.

"No more spooky stuff," his child said. "Time for a story."

Peter could see the rest of Michael's room in his periphery, but he didn't dare take his eyes off the boy. He lifted trembling hands to his son's cool face, splaying out his fingers to touch as much of him as possible.

"Michael?"

"C'mon, tell me a story."

Peter pulled him close and felt how frail he was, how small. Outside, snowflakes fell like little angels.

It had snowed his last week—Michael's last week.

"Ow. Too tight."

"I'm sorry."

"Story, story," the boy said as he wriggled out of the hug.

This is a dream. I'm in a dream.

The thought settled Peter, and he finally smiled. His boy— his beautiful, *breathing* boy. He took the boy's small hands in his. His fingers so like his own, the red marks on his arm so like his mother's.

"Story!" Michael insisted.

"All right, all right. Which one, kiddo?" Peter had a million of 'em.

"I want a new one."

"You got it." He settled in next to Michael and lay down, looking up at him. The boy watched with hollow, expectant eyes.

Peter suddenly realized he couldn't come up with a single idea. Not a shred of a story.

"Go on, Daddy."

"Gimme a sec…" One suddenly came to mind, and he ran with it. "On a hot summer day in the middle of June, Iggy Ostrich turned to his friends and said, 'I believe I could go for an ice-cold cherry popsicle!'"

Michel tilted his head and frowned.

"No, tell the other one."

"Which one is that, Michael?"

The boy leaned in. He put his hand on Peter's, chilling it.

"The *new* one. The one about the broken bird."

The boy's words stopped him cold. "I don't…how do you know about that?"

"Tell how it flopped, Daddy. Tell how it flopped around!"

Peter sat up. His vision blurred momentarily, and he felt as if he might fall off the bed.

"Tell it!"

The falling snow had turned black, like ash.

"Tell it!"

Peter scrambled backward, willing himself away from the boy.

Black liquid, thick as blood, began trickling from Michael's nose. He touched the dark flow with his fingers and examined it. He held out his hand for his father.

"I'm messy!" the boy screamed.

"This never happened," Peter whispered.

The blackness poured from Michael's nose and mouth, soaking his shirt, the bed—moving like a living stain toward Peter's feet.

"I'm messy!"

"This never happened!"

CHAPTER 15

The software froze. The cursor disappeared, replaced by a spinning pinwheel.

"Michael!"

A second later, the audio program vanished from the screen.

Peter frantically clicked on an icon and the program reloaded. It attempted to open the last file saved before once more balking and dying.

Authorization Error: Vocable cannot run because it is corrupted. Please try reinstalling the product.

"No…"

Try as he might, Peter couldn't get the program to open.

He jumped up and abandoned the booth. He took the stairs two at a time and shoved open the back door. Peter shielded his eyes from the glaring sun as he circled the pond, willing the adrenaline from his system.

What the hell was that?

The question propelled him forward, around and around and around.

Round and round the rugged rock the ragged rascal ran…

Peter finally stopped to catch his breath.

Michael! He had seen him, touched him…

Not Michael. Not real.

His heart said different. It cried out for the boy, urging him back down into the basement. Back to the bed where his son lay screaming.

No! Not real!

He stared across the pond—the house was reflected on its surface, upside-down and undulating. Picking up a large rock, Peter stepped forward. He threw it, scattering the reflection into giggling ripples.

No.

The spell—or dream or whatever it was—was broken. The heaviness lifted, the howling grief silenced. The world normalized with alarming alacrity. A distant truck blasted its horn, putting a period to the episode.

This is what comes of remembering.

The thought hit Peter hard. He had done this to himself, jumped—too quickly, perhaps—back into the pool of memories where Michael lay buried. The same had happened to Hannah, her *bad day* the result of wading back into the depths of her sorrow.

Perhaps this was *his* bad day.

"I'm either going back in there, or I'm standing in this yard for the rest of my life," he said aloud. "What's it going to be, Peter?"

As soon as he had said it, he had his answer. He moved toward the house, hesitantly at first but gaining speed as his resolve kicked in.

"I'm coming in!" he called as he opened the door.

He marched down the stairs and headed straight for the room, for the booth, ignoring the tricks his eyes tried to play, coming so quickly as he did from sunlight to shadow.

Peter threw open the door to the audio booth and sat. "I'm getting back to work, Michael," he said, his voice muffled by the soundproofing.

And as soon as he had said the name, Peter laughed. There was no humor in it, only release. It was laugh or cry, and so he laughed as he searched his computer, located the Vocable folder on his external hard drive and reinstalled the program.

His hands were so cold.

Shut it down.

I should have stayed with him.

Now.

He opened the program. It went through its initialization phase, then offered up a new project window. Peter closed the window, located the *Iggy Ostrich* sample file and opened it.

He zoomed out on the timeline so he could see the full length of the waveform—the rises and falls of his voice laid out like a landscape.

He played the final seconds of the track to confirm what his eyes had already surmised.

The glitch was gone.

Just like my boy.

With practiced movements, Peter selected the entire track, deleted its contents and closed the program.

* * *

By the time Hannah came back, Peter had taken the Vocable program out for a spin, assured himself that all was in working order, loaded the bulk of the books to his tablet and shut down the system. All ready to attack the thirteen-week contract with gusto.

"If that's okay with you, Michael?" he said. When he received no answer, he closed up the booth, latched it tight, shut off the lights and headed upstairs.

Hannah was loaded down with Bourne Farm Outfitter bags.

"Why haven't you told me about this place until now?" Hannah asked, holding up her purchases. "I've died and gone to honky heaven."

For the next hour, she proceeded to treat him to a private runway show, parading a slew of low-rise jeans and variations on Daisy Duke tops, all the while lubing up her lips with a shiny, fruity gloss. Peter could smell it from where he sat.

"This flannel, I can tie up around my midriff," she said, demonstrating by doing just that. "I got some tanner. My belly is as white as a sheet."

She was a knockout in every outfit. She combined work shirts, flannel and denim like an artist, thwarting their utilitarian purpose and bending them to her will. The light that had sparked when they first stepped foot in the house was on full floodlight display now. She was alive and electric. And she was sexy as hell.

"I'm not going to lose you to some bubba in a cowboy hat, am I?" he asked.

She responded by pulling a straw cowboy hat of her own out from her stash of bags. "I hope not. Guess you'll have to brand me."

Such brazen talk was rare from his wife, but when she got into it, he knew better than ignore her. He rose from the chair where he'd watched her redneck fashion show and went to her. He tipped her hat back on her head. "Can I have this dance?"

"You can have more than that," she said and pressed her lips to his. Her kiss was warm and wild and strawberry.

* * *

That night he dreamed of the bird.

He was in Manhattan, riding his bike past Union Square on his way downtown. There was no traffic on the streets—no taxis to dodge, no pedestrians to avoid. It was smooth sailing as far as the eye could see.

The bird walked out of the ground floor of a building to his left and stopped to watch him as he rode by, scratching and pecking at the sidewalk in search of food. It was the bird...but it *wasn't* the bird—such was the world of dreams. It looked more like a man in a bird suit. Oversized wings, jutting beak.

As he whizzed past, eager to be rid of the thing, the bird/not bird spoke but a single word.

Messy.

CHAPTER 16

Hannah woke with a singular purpose. Buoyed by Peter's response to her new wardrobe—and to the other things he had offered that night—she arose with a hope the likes of which she hadn't felt since her husband had told her they were giving up the apartment and heading west.

She tiptoed to the bathroom, hoping to allow Peter a few more minutes of sleep—he'd tossed and turned all night. The floor creaked with each step. Peter was usually the first one up. He preferred doing his work before the sun rose. There was always a certain smug 'I did it' look on his face when they sat for their morning coffee, and he told her that he had already reached his daily recording goal. Those were good days. And they had been few and far between lately.

Not that she understood her husband's business—not really. He would disappear into his booth for days at a time and come out only for hot tea and plain bread—very Dickensian fare. When finished with a book, he'd plop in front of the TV, channel surf until he found some old movie he'd seen a billion times and proceed to down half a six-pack. He was the artist of their little duo. The sensitive one, the performer, the thinker. She was the pragmatist, the doer. Between the two of them, they had all the bases covered. That was until Michael got sick—then, none of their skills seemed to be worth a damn.

Still, what Peter did in that booth of his remained a mystery to her. It paid the bills, afforded them insurance through his union. But she could tell that the hours alone took their toll on him. At times, he likened it to solitary confinement.

During the weeks before Michael's death, Peter had practically lived in his booth. He took on every project they offered. It gave the minutes she saw him a frantic quality.

Michael had sensed it too. Once, he had pulled her close and said, "Do you know why Daddy's so busy? It's because he doesn't want to see me."

Hannah had assured him that was *not* the case. "He just wants to make sure we have the money to pay the bills, sweetie," she had said, knowing it to be but a half-truth. For Peter *had* avoided Michael at the end. And as much as she hated to admit it, she resented him for it. She'd had nowhere to hide, no tiny room to duck inside when things got bad—when the first of the diapers appeared, when the nurse gave her IV lesson, when the morphine shots began.

But hadn't she found him many nights curled up beside the boy in his hospital bed, a stack of books strewn about them both? Hadn't it been Peter who held Michael as he wretched and gasped in reaction to a new medication? And hadn't it been Peter who was with him at the end? The night of Michael's goodbye?

The bathroom was a rustic affair, to say the least. A giant clawfoot tub, orange-streaked with rust sat next to the window. A hand-held showerhead, a recent addition, lay in its cradle. She adjusted the water to her liking—scalding hot—and slipped out of her t-shirt and undies.

As she showered, she recalled the previous night. Peter's primal urgency. The squeak and groan of the inflatable bed. It was a welcome tussle, welcome after such a long dry season. But something about it also worried her. Peter had brought something else to the table other than his love and lust—he had brought a nervous energy she couldn't quite place. And she could have sworn at times that he was using her to hide from the world. Hide inside of her.

She let the water play across her belly and examined the stretch marks. Would they ever go away? They had faded over the years, but she had a feeling she would wear them until her dying day. Hopefully, the tanning lotion she'd bought would help to cover them.

Hannah toweled off and dressed. The air was cool and raised gooseflesh on her arms and legs as she walked past Peter asleep in the bed and picked her way down the stairs to the kitchen.

As she started the coffee, she thought, *It's like we're camping.* And it was. The fridge was partially filled with hotdogs and hamburger patties. The only thing missing were marshmallows. And bears.

Today, she'd jump back into the fray, and that was comforting. Pouring beers, mixing drinks—it was probably as old hat as Peter's recording was for him. They both had routines to fall back on, to get them through the newness of this all. And maybe that was enough right now. Tomorrow was tomorrow's problem.

The coffee maker spat, letting her know that the pot was full.

I'm never going to end up like them, she thought. *Like Peter's parents. I'll throw myself in front of a train first.* The idea caught her unaware, but she knew it to be true. Why such morbid musings on such a lovely morning?

She walked down the hall and called up the stairs to the second floor.

"Coffee's on!"

After a moment, she heard him stirring, and a moment after that, they were sharing their coffee on the front porch.

* * *

The red cowboy boots she'd pulled from the moving box had won out over all she'd seen at Bourne Farm Outfitters. Granted, if she'd bought them new, she'd have to break them in. But her reliable old red boots gave her an extra boost when she put them on. Like she was ready to do battle.

Hannah prepped her outfit as Peter prepped his text. She thought about donning her new skinny jeans but, as it was still unseasonably warm, opted for the cutoffs she'd found on the half-price rack.

Once dressed, coiffed, primped and primed, she took a look at herself in the full-length mirror that had once adorned the hallway closet in their apartment.

What she saw made her wince.

I'm trying too damn hard.

She ditched the shorts for the jeans, made sense of her teased hair and buttoned an extra button on her Wrangler shirt.

Better.

It felt nice to get dolled up, but she had veered into Halloween costume territory. *Sexy Bartender Costume - $14.99!* Better to play it cool and suss out the atmosphere at her new gig before going whole hog.

As she applied the final touches to her makeup, she remembered something Peter had said.

"I think you're amazing."

Yeah, she thought as she finished lining her eyes, *I am.*

* * *

"Why do you have to go in so early?" Peter asked.

The truth of the matter was that she *didn't* have to go in early, but she figured she'd give Peter a few extra hours alone to record.

Besides, she could use some time alone to call back Lillian Dann. The woman had left her two messages about purchase options for the house—financing and such. And what the hell? Peter had his work; she had hers. Why not at least hear the woman out?

"I told Riggs I'd help him do inventory," she lied.

"Well, make sure you flip him the bird for me," Peter said.

"Will do."

He waved her over for a kiss. She grabbed the keys and her coffee and headed for the Prius.

The day was cool and threatening rain. The wind was picking up.

She checked herself in the mirror. She'd have to reapply before she got to work. His kiss had smeared her lipstick.

"Oof," she said and started the car. "Messy."

* * *

The Blind Rock was locked up tight when Hannah arrived. She tried both front and back doors to no avail. She was about to call the number Riggs had given her when the man himself appeared around the corner, dressed in a bowling shirt and cargo shorts.

"Damn! I thought it was supposed to be warmer today," he said, dancing in place. "Open up, quick."

"I don't have a key," Hannah said.

Riggs nodded. "A thing to be rectified posthaste. Where'd you get that outfit? You are going to rake in the tips, sister."

Hannah went red. "Too much?"

"Too much is never enough at the ole' Rock. Scoot over, honeypie. Lemme at that door."

Once they were inside, Riggs worked his magic with the lights. Soon, neon signs flickered to life, turning the place from a dark shithole to garishly lit shithole. The bar smelled like sour beer and fried food. Hannah was smitten immediately.

"The Rock is in business!" Riggs crowed. The row of video poker machines warbled their approval.

"Where do I…do I have to clock in?" Hannah asked.

"Hell no. But what you can do is get me a bunch of ice from downstairs. I always lay in extra down in the freezer for Saturday nights. That is unless you wanna wait for Devon, he's our bar back today. Dumb as a nub, but the girlies like him. Used to be on the wrestling team over at the college until they figured out how dumb he was. Poor kid couldn't put two thoughts together if he tried. But I got a soft spot for hard-luck stories."

Hannah raised her eyebrow. "Like mine?"

Riggs threw up his hands. "Honeypie, hiring you was one of my more mercenary decisions. Between your hips and my hops, we're gonna clean up!"

"Oh, really?"

"Guaranteed!"

"You've got a lot of energy for nine-thirty in the morning," Hannah said.

"That's because I'm still a wee bit drunk from last night. Nothing a Bloody Mary won't cure."

Hannah nodded. "Extra ice is downstairs?"

"Downstairs."

* * *

By the time Hannah returned with the ice, Riggs had his first two customers of the day—two portly, old fellows had plopped down in the middle of the bar.

"Yo, Hannah!" Riggs said. "This is Killer and T-Bone. Boys, this is Hannah."

Hannah set down her buckets of ice and offered her hand. "Fellas."

The men grunted their hellos, but neither took her hand.

"Set you up with the regular?" Riggs asked. The men nodded and grunted again. "Two 7 and 7's, comin' up," Riggs said, leaping into action. He deftly poured the old men's drinks and set them in front of them. "What do you wanna hear?"

"Waylon," drawled the chubbier of the two, the man Riggs had called Killer.

"Waylon it is," Riggs answered. He flipped on the sound system and tapped a song list on his phone. "I've Always Been Crazy" blared from the speakers. "Loud enough for you?"

Killer nodded, and the two proceeded to drink in unison.

Riggs pulled Hannah aside.

"Whatever the old boys want, it's on the house."

"Seriously?"

"For reals. Killer there does my taxes for free, and T-Bone got me out of a DWI. Twice." He leaned in, lowering his voice. "They're a couple, you know."

Hannah balked. "No. Really?"

"For the past twenty years. Ever since their wives went belly up," Riggs said with a smile. "But so much as mention it, and they'll punch your lights out."

Hannah looked back at the two old fellows sipping their drinks and shrugged. Not quite the Saturday crowd she had expected.

That would change as soon as the first of the college students started trickling in through the door.

CHAPTER 17

For most of the morning, Peter avoided the basement, opting instead to prep *Iggy Ostrich* on his tablet in the bedroom.

He lounged in his Hell's Kitchen t-shirt and pajama bottoms, flipping through the book and assigning voices to Iggy and his menagerie of friends.

"I'm Iggy Ostrich!"

"I'm Terrence Snake."

"I'm Rowdy Rac-ac-ac-ac-coon!"

Once he finished, he moved on to Jennifer Hornblum's magnum opus, *Max's Attic.*

"Wow, sis! This attic goes on and on and on."

"I want to go back downstairs, Max!"

Good for you, little girl. I sure don't.

Peter tapped his email and dawdled, sending junk mail to the trash and ignoring messages from friends. There was a friendly reminder from Flatiron Audio to update his hours every Friday, a nudging reminder that he was on the clock.

He pulled the cord from the tablet, its battery filled to the brim. He should get to work, hit the books. Instead, he opened the photo library, and the last picture views appeared on the screen.

It was a shot of Hannah and Michael on the top deck of the ferry to Weehawken, where Hannah's parents lived. Mother and son both laughed at some secret joke, heads thrown back and eyes shut. It was his favorite photo of all time.

He flipped to the next, and Hannah's parents appeared. Merv with his silver hair and cigar, Alice with her hand out, trying to stop him from taking her picture. Good people. And how they loved Michael.

Swiping forward, he came to the point when the archived photos no longer contained pictures of people, only snapshots of scribbled grocery lists and prescription labels. Then, one final photo taken by accident—his own face staring blankly into the lens, washed out by the unexpected flash. The ceiling behind him was ornate metal tile. The funeral home.

He was about to shut the tablet off and head downstairs for some more coffee when three more photos appeared in the queue—uploaded from his phone, no doubt.

Peter opened the first.

A crayon drawing lying on a cement floor appeared on the screen. He recognized it instantly—one of the drawings he'd found downstairs. Same hand, same subject.

The picture was a scribbled man, his arms raised in anger over a scribbled woman.

Was this another accidental photo?

The tablet vibrated in his hands, and the photo changed. Another drawing popped up. This time, the crayon man was holding the woman aloft. A torrent of red crayon poured from her mouth. Like the previous photo, Peter could see the surface on which the drawing lay.

That's the main staircase.

A waft of rancid meat filled the room. His gorge rose, and he coughed sour coffee spittle. He squeezed his eyes shut, willing his stomach to calm down.

In his self-imposed darkness, he struggled to breathe through his mouth, but he could *feel* the stench in the air all around him. Like a dead animal unearthed. Like rot.

He breathed in and out. In. Out.

A massive thump rocked the house.

He threw open his eyes. The room was dark.

He looked to the window. Outside the sky was grey.

What the—?

He checked his tablet for the time and found that the battery was down to twelve percent.

It was 8:09 pm.

He'd lost nine hours.

Jesus…

A third image illuminated the screen. The crayon man was laughing, hands thrown up to the sky, his crayon woman sinking into the frantic blackness of a scribbled pond.

The drawing was lying on a wooden floor, the corner of a patterned sheet just in view. The same patterned sheet that now covered his feet.

The rot hung in the air like a mist.

Peter slowly crawled to the foot of the bed, working up the courage to peer over the edge.

Don't be there.

He looked down at the floor. No drawing.

He breathed a sigh of relief.

Peter was about to rise when a man walked past the open door.

He froze.

CHAPTER 18

"This sucks," shouted a girl at the bar as she devoured the free pretzels Hannah had set out.

"I know," replied her date, a thin kid with a buzz cut. "We should have gone to Wild Ed's. They've got fifty beers on tap."

The girl checked her phone. "Shit, it's already eight."

Hannah watched as Devon the bar back hovered next to the rack of potato chips, straightening the bags. Drink orders had gone from scant to zip.

She spied Riggs hiding over by the pool tables and walked on over. She hitched her thumb back at the pitiful number of patrons at the bar. "What's going on? I've had half a dozen kids leave. Even your buddies, Killer and…"

"T-bone."

"They took off. What gives?"

Riggs pointed to a clutter of band posters taped, tacked and stapled to the wall.

"The Bright Chiefs were supposed to play tonight. Local group, nothing but covers. They bring 'em in and keep 'em in."

"And?" Hannah said, not liking where this was going.

"One of the kids told me the band split up last week. Artistic differences or money trouble, who knows. So, I just called them. Long story short, we don't have a band tonight."

"Okay, that's bad."

"It's *beyond* bad. The Rock is *the* place to hit once you're back on campus. Saturday before classes, this crowd expects a big blowout. No band, no fuckin' sales. Word's gonna get around—I'm gonna lose 'em all to that new joint in Galesburg or Doc's over in Oquawka. Shit! We gotta do something. Quick."

Hannah looked back at the bar. A dozen or so girls lazed about while half as many guys played video poker or checked their phones.

"That's a good ratio," she said.

"Huh?"

"I'm going to give something a try. Always worked back in the day. You don't happen to have a drinking song playlist, do you?"

Riggs grinned. "Just so happens I do."

He fiddled with his phone and Tracy Byrd's "Watermelon Crawl" kicked in over the speakers.

"Crank it."

Hannah undid the two top buttons on her shirt and stalked back to the bar. One by one, she scooped the bowls of pretzels out from under the college kids' noses.

"Hey!" a bleached blonde squealed.

Hannah grabbed a stack of shot glasses and set them up in a row down the bar. She grabbed the largest shaker she could find, threw in a handful of ice and proceeded to make a massive drink in time with the music. Sloe gin, amaretto, Southern Comfort.

She snatched the soda gun from its holster, stepped up on the beer cooler and shot orange juice down into the pitcher, tapping out time with a red cowboy boot.

Every boy at the bar had their eyes on her, and that included Riggs.

Hannah bent down and capped the shaker. She caught Riggs' eye and winked.

"Sonofabitch," he whispered.

With moves learned over years tending bar in the roughest Jersey dives, Hannah hypnotized the males in the room, raising the ire of the females. She shook the shaker left, she shook the shaker right—she had them all on a string.

Two young guys stepped in the front door and froze. "Damn," one said.

Pulling out moves she hadn't tried in a decade, Hannah heel-toed it down the length of the bar, pouring high-flying shots as she went. Only one missed its mark, and that was because a kid in a John Deere hat leaned over and caught it in his mouth.

"This round's for the guys," Hannah said, raising the shaker. "Here's to you, boys. It's Alabama Slammer time! Five…four…three…"

There was a mad rush for the shot glasses, and by the time Hannah reached zero, the drinks were down and gone.

She locked eyes with buzz cut and sauntered over to him. "Only a little left," she said. The boy held out his empty shot glass, and she deftly poured the last of the liquid, filling it to the brim.

Wait for it…

As if on cue, buzz cut's date grabbed the shot from his hand and downed it.

"Whoo!" the girl cried, covering up the burn.

113

Hannah turned back to Riggs and gave him the volume up signal with her thumb. It took him a second to translate, but his timing proved advantageous, the sound system belting out Gretchen Wilson as the next song started up.

Buzz cut's date clambered up onto the bar.

"Whoo!" she said, echoing herself.

Wait for it...

A second ignored girl hopped up and joined her. Soon, four gals were dancing on the bar.

Hannah slid off the bar and went from guy to guy.

"Don'cha wanna buy the lady a drink?"

"Two shots for the price of one."

"Now *that's* a girl who needs some Jack."

Hannah glanced over at Riggs, who stood marveling at her. Yeah, all she'd done was play on the poor girls' jealousies to sell a few drinks, but it felt so good to know she still had it. It made her smile, made her feel alive for the first time in months.

She snapped in Riggs' direction. "You gonna stand there with your thumb up your ass or are you gonna help a girl out?"

"Let's do it to it!" Riggs said. He hustled to her side and grabbed up a bottle of Jack.

CHAPTER 19

Peter stood stock-still next to the bed. Wind rattled the window behind him.

"Hello?" he said to the darkness. The darkness didn't answer.

He flicked on the overhead light. The room lit up pale and yellow.

He took a step forward, and the floor creaked. He paused, listening.

"Hello?" he said, louder this time.

Nothing.

With the bedroom light on, the world beyond the doorway had gone decidedly darker. Anything could be lurking out there.

Something was. The spoiled meat smell told him as much. The figure had glided by rapidly, but not so fast that Peter couldn't make out a few details. The man was small in stature—wiry. He was dressed in grey work pants and a flannel shirt. His face was as ashen as stone.

He had dead eyes.

He hadn't seen Peter. Peter didn't know how he knew this—he just...knew it. The same way he knew that if he stepped through the doorway and into the heart of the house, he *might* see him. *Could* see him.

He hesitated a moment longer, then headed for the door. He stepped out onto the landing overlooking the flight of steps to the foyer. He heard the rustling of paper below, like leaves caught in the wind, but definitely paper. Was it the drawings fluttering about? Waiting for him to come on down?

He threw on the light over the stairs, and they descended before him. He walked slowly, picking his way down, eyes and ears open and alert.

As soon as he hit the foyer, he heard a splintering crash behind him, and he whirled about. The sound had come from down the hallway.

From the kitchen.

He knew this because the kitchen light was on, casting its green glow into the hallway.

Peter wished he had a pot and pan in hand so he could bang away, New Year's Eve-style to let whatever was in the kitchen know he was heading its way.

Screw that. Give me a gun. A big ass gun.

He approached the kitchen and saw the glint on the floor too late to stop. Shards of glass bit into his right foot, and he recoiled.

Raising his leg, Peter pulled the pieces of broken glass from his sole—three in all, the last one the deepest. He rubbed the wounds briskly with his thumb, smearing blood. Watching for glass, he took a tentative step. His wounds stung.

Picking his way around the scattered pieces, he rounded the kitchen door. The brown, plastic handle of the coffeemaker lay in a pile of curved glass shards sitting in the remains of their morning pot of joe.

The coffee was black in the flickering fluorescent light. And it was everywhere—splashed across the linoleum floor, dripping down the fridge. Like a mini crime scene.

The dead scent was stronger here. It rose from the coffee-splattered floor, seeped from the wallpapered walls.

Like the whole house is rotting.

A door slammed, and Peter knew instantly it was the door to the basement. He could hear it open and close, over and over—wooden claps daring him to investigate. To go see what all the fuss was about.

He stepped through the obstacle course of broken glass and headed toward the back of the room, leaving bloody footprints in his wake.

When he stepped through the doorway into the back room and switched on the light, he caught the basement door slamming shut.

All was quiet. Peter instantly regretted everything—coming to Illinois, moving into the house…

Coming downstairs.

There was a knock on the basement door, and Peter leaped back. It came again, quiet but rapid tapping. He heard a muffled voice but couldn't make out the words. Should he approach? Should he *open* the door?

Fuck that noise.

Still, Peter found himself moving toward it. With a hand not his own, he reached out and grabbed the doorknob.

CHAPTER 20

The door flew open, striking the boy in the head and sending him tumbling down the stairs. He felt his back crack against the steps as he fell, sending shocks of pain up his spine. He hit the cement floor with a whomp, the impact robbing him of his breath.

The Old Man spat. "Serves you right, you little shit."

The boy gasped for air. "Daddy…"

"I warned you, didn't I? I need my shuteye. Didn't I warn you?"

"Don't." It was all the boy could do to form the word.

The Old Man took a step down. "Be quiet, I told you. You know I told you. Don't listen. Just like your mama. You don't never listen."

The man's hands went to his belt. He undid it and drew it out slowly, making sure the motion lasted, making sure the boy saw what was coming for him. He doubled it over itself and made the leather *snap.*

"Thinkin' maybe its time…"

"Daddy."

"Time for you to go. Let me sleep. Leave me be."

The Old Man took a step down.

The boy's hand went to his head and came away wet. "I'm hurt!"

"Yeah," the Old Man said. "Time."

As he gave the belt another *snap*, the Old Man's grey lips pulled back in a skeletal grin.

"Time to see your mama."

He lurched down to the next step.

The boy screamed. And as he did so, he could feel the cold darkness gather around him. Pressing against him, urging him upward.

Whispers whistled in his ears, sharp and painful, making him wince.

Up.

Forcing him to his knees…

Get up.

To his feet…

Yes.

Pushing him forward.

Yes!

He felt the blackness brush against him, *through* him. Like silk.

Let…

Like breath.

Me…

Like death.

IN.

"Yes!" the boy cried.

The darkness chittered and caroused with glee. Blackness poured into his mouth. It flowed in through his ears, through his eyes, through his nose, burrowing deep inside. Filling him up.

With a final gasp, the boy breathed in the last of it. He felt the thing coil within him. And then, he was running for the stairs.

CHAPTER 21

Peter yanked open the door, and the sight of the grey man standing below him on the stairs made him cry out.

The man, the *thing* had its back turned. A waft of charnel stench hit Peter hard, and this time he couldn't stop his stomach from emptying.

He quickly recovered, bracing himself against the doorway. The man was solid one moment, shimmering and insubstantial the next. His skin was sallow as death. His clothes hung like rags from his withered frame.

He...it... Peter's mind raced, for it was both man and thing at the same time. Living yet dead—here, yet not here.

"Time!" the man rasped. His voice was dust and decay.

Peter screamed.

The grey man lowered the belt, and to Peter's horror, he turned back to him. *Saw* him.

"Holy shit!" Peter couldn't move.

The man's face... oh, God! His face!

It was the face of a corpse.

He felt a rush of wind rising up the stairs. The man felt it too and turned.

A boy, no older than his Michael, leaped up out of the darkness and wrapped his arms around the grey man's neck.

The step on which the man stood—the one Peter's father had repaired but hadn't matched—cracked beneath their combined weight. The wood split underfoot, and the grey man dropped like a condemned man at the gallows.

He fell fast, then stopped with a jerk.

The boy toppled back a few steps and grabbed hold of the railing, bracing his fall.

The grey man gurgled.

Heart pounding, threatening to rip from his chest, Peter leaned out to look upon the scene below.

Only the man's head remained in view, held fast by a jagged piece of wood. It pierced his jaw from beneath and jutted from his mouth like a hook, dangling him, his feet kicking below. He tried to speak, but his dry tongue only clucked.

Then, he went still.

Peter looked past the dead man at the boy, who crouched panting on the stairs below. Their eyes locked.

The boy's mouth opened, and the blackness poured out, rushing, screaming up the stairs toward him.

It encircled him, smothering him. Pressing close. Squeezing tight. Smelling him. Tasting him.

Ahh!

Peter wrenched himself free from the thing. The next thing he knew, he was falling.

CHAPTER 22

Peter roused a few moments later, coughing up dust. He was face down on the basement floor. His jaw hurt, and the palms of his hands hurt from breaking his fall.

The boy was gone. The grey man was gone. The broken step was intact.

"Jesus," Peter whispered.

"Hello-oo?" came a voice from upstairs.

Hannah!

Peter scrambled to his feet. "Stay right there!" he called to her.

He bounded up the stairs.

"What the hell?" Hannah said, her voice coming from the kitchen.

Peter rushed to the doorway and stopped short.

Hannah stood with the coffee pot in her hand. The liquid had boiled down to sludge, and the glass was scorched. "Has this thing been on all day?"

He stared at the pot, seeing it shattered on the floor, seeing it whole in her hand.

"I..."

"What in the world happened to you? You're a mess, Peter."

He shook his head, trying to gain his bearings. "We've got to get out of here."

"What are you talking about?"

Peter stepped forward and grabbed her by the arm. "Come on."

He hadn't meant to pull her as hard as he did. The jolt made her stumble. The pot broke free from her grip and tumbled to the floor where it exploded in a spray of coffee and glass.

"What the hell?"

Undeterred, Peter dragged his wife down the hallway and toward the front door.

"Let me go, Peter!"

He wrenched open the door and pulled her out into the night. Hannah jerked her arm and stepped free.

"What is going on with you?"

Peter stammered, trying to land on an explanation and finding none. "Where's the car?"

"Peter, you're scaring me."

He looked past her and found the Prius sitting parked next to a gnarled tree.

"What's happening?"

Peter motioned to the car. "I'll tell you. But in the car."

Hannah glared at him but complied. She walked over to the car and got in the driver's side, robbing him of the option to hit the gas and leave.

As Peter stepped onto the gravel drive, he realized that he was still barefooted; he also realized that the wounds on his right foot were still there.

He slid into the passenger seat beside her, closed and locked the door.

Hannah sat behind the wheel, arms folded. "Well? Spit it out." Her words were harsh, but there was concern on her face. This was new territory for them. Peter didn't freak out—he just didn't.

"I saw something," he said, laughing maniacally inside because he hadn't seen *something*, he had seen *many, many* things, each more horrifying than the last. "Inside. I saw something."

"What kind of something?" Hannah asked. She was still holding herself tight.

"I don't know how to…" He fumbled with his thoughts. His mind, perhaps unwilling to revisit the terror he'd just experienced, instead focused in on his wife's breathing. It was heavy and thick. Was that tequila on her breath?

Hannah reached out and put her hand on his arm. "This isn't you, Peter. You're…Jesus Christ, you're a bit nuts right now. Hell, you're a *lot* nuts. Just talk to me, sweetie."

He opened his mouth and felt the blackness laugh at him.

She won't believe you.

"Yes, she will," he said.

"Who will what?" Hannah asked. She touched his face. "I think you had a nightmare. I think you're still half in it. You're eyes…they don't look right."

"I saw a boy…"

Tell her, and she'll leave you. Tell her, and she's gone.

Peter shifted in his seat, and the absurdity of it crashed down around him. Not that he doubted what had happened— oh, no—it had. He was certain of it. But the insanity of trying to distill the encounter into terms his wife could digest was growing more obvious by the minute.

Keep it...

He felt tears well up in his eyes.

Secret.

"Our boy?" Hannah asked.

"Yes," Peter lied, and in that lie, decided to protect her from the truth. They weren't alone in the house. No, not alone at all.

His tears began to drop, rolling down his face with abandon.

"Oh, honey," Hannah said, dropping her guard. She leaned over and took him in her arms as sobs began to rack his body. "I see him every day."

Peter let her hold him, there in the car in the pitch black night. Then he let her lead him back into the house and up the stairs to the bedroom where he'd seen the grey man. And when she fell into bed next to him and her night talk commenced, he moved to the foot of the bed and sat there, waiting and watching. Keeping silent vigil over her.

* * *

When the first streaks of red began to lighten the sky, Peter rose, having perched motionless throughout the night.

He put on a pair of pants and shoes and fished the car keys out of Hannah's purse. It was stuffed with one-dollar bills.

He slipped out of the room. Downstairs, he cleaned up the broken glass and mopped up the coffee, making sure to find every last splinter.

This task complete, he walked deliberately to the basement door and swung it open—musty air and nothing more. He took a few steps down and tested his father's step. The repair felt stronger than the steps above and below it.

Satisfied that the morning had quieted the house, he hopped into the Prius—thankful for its silent start—and headed off down the drive.

The practical part of his brain told him that the Shop-a-Lot would be open and more than likely had coffee pot replacements in stock, but as he turned off onto the highway that circled Maple City, driving away from the grocery store, he realized that he was heading somewhere else altogether.

The drive took him around the boundaries of the town. Past the Intermission Motor Lodge, past Primeland and the smell of charred bacon. He drove on, looping past the old municipal airport and the fairgrounds where roadies had raised the Ferris wheel and carnies had raised their tents in anticipation of the Fall Festival crowds. Lights on rides blinked as workers tested the electricity—fellow early risers on this cool, autumn day.

Turning right, Peter rode past the Maple City Cemetery where his parents had their plots. His father had bought them from a local fellow who was having a hard time making sales. After his father's purchase, the man was flooded with orders. Friends of his father, mostly. Whatever was good enough for Big Bear was good enough for them.

Someday, they all lie together, Peter thought. *The whole lot of them.*

He headed down neighborhood streets, avoiding the school buses that had started to appear. By the time he reached Applegate, he had counted fourteen.

Recommended visiting hours were 8:30 am – 10:00 pm, but no one hassled him as he made his way to room 16. He found his father asleep in his chair, footrest up. The old fellow hadn't even changed into his PJs.

The man snored something awful, and the sound of it comforted Peter.

His mother lay curled in a question mark, balled up under layers of blankets. He leaned over her. The skin on her face was translucent as if she were made of wax.

Peter pulled up a chair and sat next to his mother's bed, but he kept his eyes on his father.

"Why did you ever buy that goddamn house, Pop?" he asked. The big man only snorted and chuffed in his sleep.

* * *

Two hours later, a nurse making her morning rounds woke Peter with a gentle shake and broke the news that his mother, Myrna Larson, was dead.

CHAPTER 23

The Jansing Funeral Home was quite accommodating. After all, Herbert Jansing was an old poker buddy of Peter's father and had apparently been allowed to let a few debts slide.

"Anything for Bill," Mr. Jansing said.

Hence, the use of the larger of the two viewing rooms even though turnout was low—had it been Big Bear himself, Peter had no doubt there would have been an overflow crowd—and the allowance to have Mrs. Whittier play the organ. The old gal usually played for Turner's Funeral Home exclusively, but Mr. Jansing being an old neighbor of theirs, Peter had asked the man if he could make an exception just this once.

"Your mother had her trials," was all Mrs. Whittier said by way of condolences before taking her place at the organ to play "A Mighty Fortress is our God."

Gina showed up ten minutes before the viewing with her kids in tow. Her husband was nowhere to be seen.

"Did you bring the photos?" she asked. Peter assured her that he did. Gina had washed her hands of anything inside the house on Oak Street, save for snapshots, prom photos and the like. Peter had three boxes in the trunk of his car waiting to be transferred to her safe-keeping.

Their father sat in a chair next to the door as far as one could get from the casket up front. The odd member of the VFW would linger to chat for a moment before going in search of the best seat for the service. Otherwise, Pop just sat there fidgeting, looking like a man waiting for a bus.

Sunday and Monday had been a flurry of activity. Peter met with Mr. Moots three times to make sure the funeral came off without a hitch.

"I guarantee, this will be the last meeting we have to have before the funeral," Moots had said. The next day, he'd called to schedule another.

"My sister and her family would like to stay in the house on Oak when they fly in. Is that going to be okay?"

Mr. Moots had frowned. "Well, Lillian tells me that the college has already signed the papers. But let me make a few calls. The name Moots still has a *little* sway in this town."

He'd made his calls, and Gina was given the green light to board her and her kids at their folks' old house. Lillian Dann's crew had done a good job cleaning the place out and storing the majority of the household items. Only the beds remained.

Peter made his way over to Gina, who was busy scolding her eldest for staring at his grandmother's corpse.

"I'm worried about Pop," he said.

"We all are. Bailey, eyes in your head!"

"I mean tonight. I hate to think of him going back to that room alone after all this. You think he could stay with you?"

Gina looked at him like he was daft. "Overnight? I don't think that's a good idea, Pete."

"It'd be nice for him to be somewhere familiar."

"Not overnight. Why don't you swing him by after the cemetery? We're going to have a little spread laid out for the neighbors. Besides, I want to get an early start tomorrow. Shea's got hockey."

Peter nodded. His sister, like his mother, was a force to be reckoned with.

He spotted Hannah chatting with the minister and excused himself. The man shook his hand when he approached.

"I was saying to your wife that since your father didn't have any stories that he seemed…well, able to tell at the moment, I thought I'd offer up one of my more generalized sermons. Not cookie cutter, by any means. Something suited to the time and situation. Perhaps I'll begin with Daniel 12:1-3."

Peter thanked him, saying he'd defer to his judgment.

"Daniel it is."

Mr. Jansing nodded that they were ready to begin. Peter held up a finger, holding him off a minute.

"Have you paid your respects?" he asked Hannah.

"Yes," she said. "Have you?"

Peter took a deep breath, walked to the front of the room and peered down into the baby blue casket.

She looks fake.

And so she did. The woman's makeup had done a fine job of masking her lack of life, but it went too far in its attempt to make her look cheery. Her cheeks were overly red, so too her lips. She wore eyeshadow for the first time in her life, and her hair…

Dear God, that's a wig.

Her hands were clasped together in an imitation of serenity. To the rest of the world, she probably seemed at peace. But to Peter…

What are you doing in my room!

He touched her hand. Wasn't that the sort of thing that sons were meant to do?

Myrna Larson's eyes flew open.

No, they didn't.

She turned her head toward him.

No.

Her brightly painted lips parted, exposing her overly-white, dentured smile.

Nope.

"I think we'll get started," said the minister. Peter nodded and went to collect his father. The scratches on his arm itched terribly under his suit jacket.

* * *

After the graveside service, the dozen or so mourners took their collective leave. Hannah floated the idea of lunch at Myrna's favorite restaurant, but both Peter and Gina overruled her plan.

"I want to do what's best for Pop," he said. "I don't think a crowded restaurant's the way to go."

One look at Bill Larson in his baggy suit and tie, watching the traffic pass by the cemetery, and Hannah agreed.

The affair at the old house on Oak was barely an event at all. Gina's kids spent the majority of the time complaining about the lack of a TV while Gina guided neighbors to the meat and cheese spread from Shop-A-Lot.

Lillian Dann had put in an appearance, spending the majority of her time talking Hannah's ear off. Finally, his wife caught his eye and extracted herself from the realtor.

"What's that all about?" Peter asked.

"Nothing," Hannah said. "How are you doing?"

"Okay," he said, which wasn't a complete lie. Flatiron Audio had given him an extra week to get his first audio in due to his death in the family.

"We can cancel your contract if you'd like," Mika had said over the phone. Peter was quick to take that option off the table.

"The funeral didn't…bring up anything, did it?"

She was talking about the other night, of course. Peter's Crazed Night—the perfect complement to Hannah's Bad Day. It helped that the house had remained silent during this recent wrinkle in their lives. Had he heard so much as a peep out of it, he would have dragged Hannah out of there kicking and screaming and hauled ass down the road.

"I'm good. I swear."

But, he couldn't do that to her. As restless as his soul was, he couldn't move her again. She'd been patient during the funeral arrangements, had begged off working her shifts at the bar. Riggs had told her not to worry, that the Blind Rock was waiting for her whenever she was ready to come back.

In fact, he was here, wasn't he?

He found Riggs scarfing down shrimp doused in cocktail sauce.

"Thanks for understanding," Peter said.

"Of course, my friend," Riggs replied. "Besides, what was I going to do? Fire my moneymaker? That wife of yours knows how to squeeze gold from a lemon."

"Well put."

"Sorry about your mom. Never really got to know her, but then again, this is only the second time I've ever been in this house."

Peter scowled. "That's not true. You were over tons of times."

"Not so, monsieur. I was a frequent visitor to your backyard, it's true, but I wasn't…how shall I put this? *Welcome* inside."

It was true. Myrna, the gatekeeper, had barred the doors to his friends.

"Besides," Riggs continued. "We didn't pal up until late, you being a senior, me being a lowly frosh."

"Frosh is a college freshman."

"Is it?"

Peter looked about for his father but didn't see him. More than likely, the old fellow was wandering around the place, wondering where all his stuff went.

"Now, what was the name of that play we did together?" Riggs asked.

"Shit, I couldn't tell you."

"Ole Larson and his ten-minute memory. It was *The Cat and the Canary*, you dumb fuck." Riggs tensed, looking around at the other mourners. "Sorry, Jeez. Language."

Hannah caught his eye from across the room. She'd been deep in conversation with Gina and now waved him over.

"Hold that thought," he said to Riggs.

Peter avoided getting ensnared in conversation as he made his way to his wife's side.

"We've got a problem," Hannah said.

"It's *more* than a problem!" Gina shouted.

"Hush, Gina." Hannah's voice was steely, and it shut his sister down. It was a skill for which Peter immediately envied her.

"What's wrong?" he asked.

"Don't panic," Hannah said. "But we can't find your dad. And your sister's car is missing."

* * *

Peter's search took him all over Maple City.

He started with his father's old businesses—the dry cleaners, the car wash—all the while keeping his eye out for Gina's purple PT Cruiser.

He'd told Hannah and Gina to hold off calling 911 for half an hour to give him a chance to make an initial sweep, and his time was almost up.

Where the hell was the old guy headed?

Peter had a flash of insight and steered his way back to Jansing's Funeral Home, realizing that was literally the last place his father had seen his mother, but the place was deserted.

His phone rang. It was Hannah.

"Tell me you found him," he said.

"No, but I wanted to tell you that your sister is calling the police. You might as well come on back."

"Just what he needs today. A ride in a cop car."

"Peter, he might hit someone."

"I know."

"Come on back."

He hung up and was about to take the next left back to Oak when he spotted the PT Cruiser.

You gotta be shittin' me.

The car was racing away from him, but Peter could tell it was a match. He made a wildly illegal maneuver through a red light to get on the car's tail, and the chase was on.

* * *

Peter's father outpaced him for several miles, and if the situation weren't so dire, weren't so downright *sad*, Peter might have seen the humor in the race—a PT cruiser versus a Prius.

Fortunately, the ride steered clear of neighborhoods and schools, his father sticking to the main roads, determined it seemed to get the hell outta Dodge.

The train tracks on the edge of town slowed his father enough that Peter managed to pass him. With total disregard for the Prius, he swerved to the right, blocking his father's path. Luckily, the old man hit the brakes.

Peter hopped out of the car and strode, state trooper-style, to the PT Cruiser's driver's side window. He rapped on the glass.

His father rolled down the window. "Yes?"

"Where are you going, Pop?"

"Pete?"

"Yeah, it's Pete."

Peter reached in through the window, turned off the ignition and retrieved his sister's keys.

"You had us a bit worried. You wanna get out of the car?"

His father didn't budge. "She's dead. Right? She's dead?"

"That's right, Pop."

"I knew that." His father's face wrinkled in sudden sorrow. "I knew she was. But I don't want her to be."

Peter's breath caught in his throat at the childlike truth of the statement. At the sheer honesty of it.

"She was the most beautiful gal I'd ever seen. You're sure she's gone?"

"Yeah. She is." Peter opened the door. "Come on. Let me take you home."

CHAPTER 24

Peter returned his father to Applegate. After a brief chat with the social services office about next steps—new roommate, grief counseling and such—he bolted for the front door.

He called Hannah. "I'll pick you up in ten so we can go get Gina's car. That work for you?"

"Don't worry about it," Hannah said through the car's speakers. "Riggs and I already took care of it. Your sister decided not to stay the night, and she wanted her car back ASAP. She can be…well, you know."

"I sure do."

"Shea ate too much cheese and got a stomach ache. And a woman from the college dropped by. I guess Mr. Moots didn't get around to telling them your sister and the kids would be squatting another day."

Peter tapped his fingers on the steering wheel. "All right, I'll see you at home."

He heard a horn honk in the distant. "I'm not there. Riggs and I are swinging by the tavern so I can pick up keys."

"You're not working today?"

"No, just getting my keys. Your sister said she wants to be on the road by three. I already said my goodbyes, but you should go on back before she leaves. Maybe you can make sure all the food gets thrown out? We don't want the folks from the college to find the same kind of mess we did."

"I'll take care of it."

"Love you."

"Love you, too."

Phone call ended, Peter headed down Pine Street on his way to Oak.

Riggs and I already took care of it.

He scratched at his forearm. The itch was getting worse.

* * *

That afternoon, after Gina had made her escape and before Hannah returned home, Peter made a beeline for his laptop.

He conducted a quick search of his narration email account and located the message he was looking for.

Ellen Marx.

Ms. Marx was the author of three books he'd narrated for Quoth Audio, a now-defunct company that had blinked out of existence before he'd seen the last of his paychecks. The author's messages had grown progressively more terse. Not directed at him, but at the producers at Quoth. When had he last heard from them? Had they paid him yet? What kind of filthy liars were these people?

Her contact info listed Iowa City as her place of residence—a major city for this part of the country. It was only two hours west of Maple City. He could be there and back before Hannah even knew he was gone.

He tried the number and was pleasantly surprised when Ellen answered.

"Yeah, who's this?"

"Hi, Ms. Marx. This is Peter Larson. I narrated your *Heartland Haunts* series a couple years back? I was wondering if I could have a moment of your time."

* * *

That night, as Peter lay in bed next to Hannah, he had an odd sensation of anticipation. True, his mothers' funeral had shaken him, but for some reason, its timing was not surprising. Myrna Larson would have hated to have him miss out on her death. She would have wanted him to be knee-deep in it.

Hannah rolled over on her side and played with his hair. "I'm sorry about your mom."

"Yeah."

He felt something tug at the back of his brain. A subtle vibration thrilled his nerves. The sensation was akin to the gut-dropping feeling of being strapped and locked into a roller coaster.

The house was stirring.

"I need the car tomorrow," he said.

"Oh, yeah?"

"I need to make a run to Galesburg. A couple of my cables are shot. I need to replace them before I start back up."

"Good you found out now. When do you plan to get back to it?"

"Later tomorrow after I get everything hooked back up," Peter said. "And you? What's your schedule."

Hannah lay on her back and stretched her neck. She raised her hands above her and laced her fingers, eentsy-weensy spider-style. "I'm scheduled for tomorrow, but I could always beg off and take a drive with you."

"No," he said, a little too quickly. "That's okay. We need the money."

"You'll have to drive me to work."

"I know."

"And pick me up."

"Yup."

She turned her head, and the lamplight caught in her eyes, making them sparkle.

"Tell me something about her."

"Mom?"

"Yeah. Just one story. From when you were little?"

Peter stared at the ceiling, and he thought the shadows froze as if suddenly aware they were being watched.

"When I was eleven, my mom took me to Lobster Shack in the Quad Cities—just her and me. We had crab and shrimp and hush puppies. She ordered extra cornbread and gave me a sip of her wine. It might have been my birthday, but I'm not sure."

Hannah nodded. "That's nice. That's a nice memory."

Peter didn't mention how Myrna had turned on a dime during the ride home, screaming at him when he threw up shrimp and cornbread all over the back seat.

"You haven't happened to come across any of your father's papers have you?"

Peter thought of the boxes marked *Personal* in the basement. "I don't think so. Like what?"

"Any paperwork your dad might have had for the house. Lillian has some interesting ideas about financing—"

"Nope. I'm kinda tired, sweetie," he said. "Can we chat in the morning?" The last thing he wanted to think about was sinking deeper roots in the place.

She squeezed his shoulder. "Sure. You want me to sing to you?"

"Yeah."

Hannah sang him a quiet, made-up tune but put herself to sleep, instead.

Peter lay awake listening to the house's bones creak, as if it were shaking off a dream, ready to wake.

CHAPTER 25

The boy bolted upright. He pressed back into the chair. His whole body started shivering, and he feared he would wet himself for the second time that night.

A thought…no, a *voice* crept into his head.

Coming in.

The door quivered as if someone was leaning against it, trying to stifle a laugh. Nails scratched against the wood.

"Dad?" the boy whispered.

The door shuddered.

"Is that you?" Knowing it was not.

Coming…

"Please don't."

Coming…

"No."

Coming…

"No!"

In.

CHAPTER 26

Peter dropped Hannah off at the Blind Rock the next morning.

"I'll give you a buzz when I'm done, okay?" she said as she got out of the car. "Might be a late one. Riggs has a Hump Day special going on."

"You call, I'll come," Peter said.

"Aren't you forgetting something?" Hannah leaned in for a smooch, and he kissed his denim-clad gal. "Always time for a kiss."

He pulled away from the curb and watched Hannah disappear into the tavern in the rearview mirror.

It troubled Peter, lying once more to his wife, but unless he could get a grip on the situation, there was no way they were staying put in Maple City.

Get a grip on the situation? Ha. You don't even know what the hell the situation is.

"Shut up," he told himself. He turned on the radio and lost himself in somnolent NPR banter as he hit Interstate 74 heading north to catch 80 West.

* * *

He pulled into a truck stop at the junction of 74 and 80 to gas up and grab a cup of *80's Best* coffee. Unfortunately, the coffee was stale, and he dumped it out the window as he merged onto the highway. Too bad. He was running on fumes in the sleep department.

He mulled over how to approach his meeting with Ellen Marx. It seemed that the woman had a hunk of grudge she'd need to get off her chest before they got down to it, and he was prepared to allow time for that. Their mutual enemy, Quoth Audio, was his *in* with her, and he needed to gain her trust before he broached the subject of the things he'd seen in the basement.

The books of hers he'd narrated were big on procedure and short on story where the subject of hauntings was concerned. This almost clinical approach may have had readers tuning out, it was just this sort of nuts and bolts approach that Peter was seeking. He wanted to nail down what was happening, confront it with the right tools and be done with it.

He started losing the radio station as he crossed the bridge into Iowa, so he turned it off. Better to concentrate and get his story straight. Not that he planned on leaving anything out, but he found certain details eluded him. Perhaps the human brain wasn't made to process such phenomena. Or maybe he'd been too damn scared to commit the nightmare to memory.

Am I being haunted?

That was probably the logical jumping off point. Although the answer seemed simple enough—*God, yes!*—he needed to approach this as he would any other problem. Otherwise, he was afraid he'd be no match for it.

Approach *this*—no match for *it*. The vague nature of his thoughts was a buffer against the truth of what he'd experienced. But all in good time. First, he had to get his ass to Iowa City.

80 West soon became a dueling ground between long-haul truckers, bus drivers and poor wretches like himself. The larger vehicles buffeted the Prius as they passed, threatening to turn him into roadkill. The car stammered a few times in the wake of the thundering behemoths, but it got him to the outskirts of the city in good time.

A sign up ahead said *Welcome to Iowa City! Home of the University of Iowa Hawkeyes.*

"Here goes nuthin'," he said as he took Exit 224 to Dubuque Street.

* * *

Peter parked in a parking garage down the street from the coffee shop and paused to check his phone. No missed calls, and the only text message was from Lillian Dann.

Love to have lunch soon with you and the missus.

Peter ignored the message and locked the car. He opted for the stairs when the elevator proved to pull double duty as a restroom for the homeless.

Stop pushing, Ms. Dann.

Java Joint—the meeting place Ellen Marx had selected— was only two blocks north, and he was thirty minutes early. Figuring he'd dispel the memory of the truck stop coffee before meeting the author, Peter stepped into the shop. The place was hopping. The mingled scents of dark roast coffee and fresh baked muffins welcomed him.

He waited in line, eyeing the last blueberry scone. When it was his turn, he rattled off his order to the short, round woman behind the counter.

"Blueberry scone and a large dark roast. Hold on…make that pumpkin spice."

The woman's face reddened beneath her Java Joint hat.

"It's you, isn't it? What the hell? I said noon."

Peter cocked his head. "Ellen?"

She's just a kid.

Ellen's voice had a flat quality that had fooled him into thinking she was middle-aged, but standing here looking at her, he guessed she was no more than twenty-five.

She pushed up her glasses and turned to the thin barista. "Cover for me, Kevin."

The young woman motioned for him to follow her to a table away from the rest of the crowd.

She pulled off her apron and cap, revealing her head-to-toe gothic attire—the look she'd planned for him to see before being taken by surprise. Her lipstick was black, as were her nails.

The only thing she's missing is the pierced eyebrow.

"How did you know it was me?" Peter asked.

"You narrated my books. I *do* have ears, you know." Sidestepping any further introduction, she pulled her phone. "What have you got to tell me, Mr. Larson?" Ellen set the phone down on the table in front of him. The memo app was already running.

"You're recording this?"

"I won't use your real name if I write it up. That reminds me…" She picked the phone back up and spoke deliberately into it. "This is Ellen Marx. I'm speaking with Peter Larson. The following interview is copyright Ellen Marx and Apparition Press, 817 East Davenport Street, Iowa City, Iowa. My interviewee concurs with my copyright."

She stuck the phone under his nose.

"Yeah, sure. This is Peter Larson, 762 150th Street, Maple City, Illinois, and I concur."

"Good." Ellen set the phone back down. "You were saying?"

Peter looked around the room. Students sat typing away on laptops; a young girl was making a mess of her hot chocolate. It seemed strange to tell his story in a setting as normal as this. Still, he did his best.

He had to double-back a number of times as the events slipped away from him. When had the drawings appeared on his tablet? Before or after he'd had the vision of Michael? Was he upstairs or downstairs when he'd first encountered the grey man?

"I'm sorry, I'm getting a little confused."

"That's all right," Ellen said. She'd remained silent as he pieced together his recollections, but now she seemed eager to interject. "Supernatural occurrences often leave those who experience them with a sense of befuddlement. Blind spots aren't at all uncommon." It sounded as if she were writing her next book already. "Besides, if you had your story down perfect, I'd be less apt to continue our conversation."

"So, you believe me?"

"I have a few questions." She leaned back and tapped her black nails on the tabletop. Peter couldn't tell if she was actually mulling over what to ask him, or if she was doing it for effect. "Number one—"

"Do you mind if I jump in here?" Peter said, stopping her. "I don't have a lot of time, and I don't have the luxury of proving myself to you. Everything I told you is true. Every word. I came here because it feels like…well, like the house is cycling up again. Like it's going back to the first track on the album. I know that doesn't make much sense, but that's the only way I know how to describe it. I'm afraid for myself; I'm afraid for my wife. So, given what I've told you, do you think you have any idea how to help me?"

Ellen picked up her phone and stopped recording.

"Do you prefer text or email?" She was busy typing away on her phone.

"Email, I guess."

Peter sat for a few minutes as the young woman in black tapped away.

Finally, she looked up. "I just sent you a list of ten things you can try along with a copy of my ebook on prayers for the dead. Why don't you give those a try and get back to me?"

Peter stuck out his hand. "Thanks. I guess we could have done this over the phone."

Ellen shook his hand perfunctorily. And then, a glimmer of surprise crossed her face, and she gripped his hand tight. Her eyes darted about as if she were watching thoughts flit by.

"When was the funeral?"

What the…?

"Your mother's. When was it?"

"Yesterday."

Her eyes danced. "And your foot. Which time did you cut it?"

Peter fumbled. "What do you mean, which…?"

"Did you cut it when you were alone in the kitchen or with your wife?"

"When I was alone. I was following the grey man—"

"You're *sure* about that?"

"I…yes, I am."

Ellen released his hand and sat back. She sniffed, clearly rattled. "That's a lot to process. I'm going to have to get back to you on that, Mr. Larson."

She rose quickly and left Peter sitting alone at the table. Donning her apron as she walked, Ellen Marx slipped back behind the counter and took the next customer's order.

Realizing that the young woman considered their meeting finished, Peter ordered a pumpkin spice latte and a mini quiche to go and was back on the road five minutes later.

CHAPTER 27

Riggs watched as Hannah filled the salt shakers in anticipation of the Hump Day crowd. Tequila shots were on special—not the good stuff but the Ballen's well variety—and they'd need plenty of limes as well.

Hannah caught him looking at her.

"What?" she said, laughing.

"Nothing. Just make sure you don't fill 'em all the way to the top."

"No?"

Riggs joined her behind the bar. She was wearing a leather vest with a Bourne Farm Outfitter t-shirt underneath. Damn, the girl could make anything look good.

"Fill one all the way to the brim," he said.

Hannah did, spilling a good portion onto the bar in the process.

"Now, cap it and give it a shake."

Hannah replaced the cap. She licked her hand and shook the shaker over it. Only a few grains of salt made it to her moistened skin.

"Too full and the salt gets stuck."

"Ah!" Hannah said.

"What usually happens next is some college kid pops the cap to try to rectify the situation, and we end up sweeping up salt for the next three days."

"That's a very good tip."

Riggs bowed. "A little morsel of knowledge courtesy of Blind Rock University."

Hannah laughed again. "Where *did* that name come from?"

"The Blind Rock? Pat, the owner, was doing some research on the property and found out that the Parker Massacre took place on this very spot. Four families of settlers wiped out 'cause they didn't see what was coming for 'em."

"Which was?"

"No one knows. Maybe natives—maybe not. Anywhoo, ole Pat liked the name, and so it stuck. Better than what the kids call this place."

"Which is?"

"Blind Drunk."

Riggs grabbed a pinch of salt off the bar and threw it over his shoulder; Hannah did likewise.

A rumble of thunder echoed from outside.

"Guess a storm's rollin' in. That bodes well for us. Rain and tequila go well together—we'll be slammed. You ready to get your Hump Day on?"

"As ready as I'll ever be."

"Thatta girl. Lemme go see if Devon stocked up on limes."

As Riggs headed for the storeroom, he stopped and looked back at Hannah. She was licking the remaining salt from her hand.

Damn!

CHAPTER 28

The rain started falling twenty miles out of Iowa City and got progressively heavier as the minutes wore on. Peter kept a firm grip on the wheel as he did his best to avoid the water pooling on the highway. The windshield wipers could barely keep up with the deluge, and the windows kept fogging up.

He'd only taken a brief glance at Ellen's suggested remedies for what he now found himself referring to as his *situation*. The first few actions were things he could have gathered from watching movies. Smudging the house with burning sage, sprinkling holy water and his favorite, simply asking the trespassers to leave.

Yeah, right. And close the door on your way out.

Ellen's further ideas were more intriguing to him. She'd given him a list of links to online videos featuring high-frequency harmonics that were intended to disrupt spiritual energy patterns, like the sonic rodent repellers they sold at Home Depot.

Another idea she pushed was employing the practice of geomancy which was, from what Peter could deduce, simply a hooky spooky version of feng shui.

Her final recommendation came in the form of a series of prayers spoken to and for the entities. Peter found these most interesting as they weren't your garden variety litanies but prayers that Ellen claimed came to her while deep in a trance. *Practical prayers* were how she described them in her note.

And you believe her?

She did *know about Mom's passing.*

She could have read about that online.

I don't think she did.

The buzz of his phone interrupted his inner dialogue. It was Hannah.

"Hey, handsome, are you in the car?"

"I am. I'm heading back from Guitar Barn over in Galesburg." His stomach curdled at the lie.

"Any luck?"

"No. I'll have to order the cables online." He could hear the bass line of a country song in the background.

"Well, be safe on the road. It's raining buckets here. Whoops! Gotta run. A bunch of soaked college kids just came through the door. I'll call when I'm done. Bring an umbrella. Love you!"

"Love you," he said, a second after she'd hung up.

A dull ache rose in his belly, and he hoped it wasn't because of the quiche. He *had* stopped off to pick up some additional audio equipment, but it wasn't from Guitar Barn, and it wasn't meant to help him record. No, Ellen's recipe for removal had given him a brainstorm, and he was eager to try it out.

He passed half of a house on the back of a trailer, its *wide load* banner whipping in the wind. He pitied the poor driver—visibility was getting worse. As he overtook the house's escort car with its flashing lights, his phone rang again. He expected Hannah but was surprised when caller ID read *Marx, Ellen*.

"Mr. Larson?" The young woman was out of breath. "I need to talk to you."

"Seems you already are, Ellen. What's up?"

A wave of rain blasted the car, causing it to shudder. Wet leaves plastered themselves against the windshield just outside the wipers' path. Peter adjusted the heat. The inside of the car had gone suddenly cold.

"I knew there was something strange about you."

I might say the same, Ms. Marx, Peter thought.

"About your aura and your story and your...what's that noise?"

"It's the rain, Ellen. I'm in the car."

"Oh. Well, I played back our interview, and I found it very disturbing. May I share it with you? I'm going to share it with you. Emailing now."

"Why the sudden urgency?"

A lightning strike up ahead lit up the sky, illuminating wind turbines in the distant fields. A rasp of static garbled Ellen's response.

"What was that again, Ellen? I lost you."

"I need to you to listen to me, Mr. Larson."

"I am."

"Did you get my email?"

Peter glanced down at his phone for a split second. Yup, there was her email.

"Yes."

"Open the file I attached."

Had the sky grown darker? Was that even possible?

"Mr. Larson?"

"I'm a bit busy staying on the road, but…sure, I'm opening it."

The attached file was an mp3. He thought he might lose Ellen if he opened the file, but apparently phones had come a long way.

"Are you playing it?"

"I am, Ellen, now shut up so I can hear it." He hadn't meant to be so brusque, but the woman was getting on his nerves.

The recording began normally enough.

This is Ellen Marx, I'm speaking with Peter Larson. The following interview is copyright Ellen Marx and Apparition Press…

"Jump to 9:08," Ellen insisted.

Peter flipped on the defroster. It was getting hard to see the road ahead.

"Hold on." Peter fumbled with the phone and managed to get somewhat close. 8:55. Ellen's voice popped up.

…mentioned that you were renting this house, is that correct?

It is.

And neither you nor your wife have any previous connection to this residence?

None.

How long have you been staying at this house?

"Yes, Ellen. I remember what I said."

"Give it a second."

A rumbling sound, like the warning growl of a guard dog, came from the phone. And the strange thing about it was that it seemed like it didn't come *only* from the phone. It felt like it set off vibrations all around him. He stopped the recording.

"What is that?"

"I'm not sure."

"Jesus, do you have a guess?"

"I do, but you're not going to like it." *Spit it out already!* "Try me."

Sweat trickled down the back of his neck. The air, which had been downright frigid a moment ago, had become hot and humid.

"I don't think you have a pure haunting scenario on your hands, Mr. Larson. I think something's latched onto you."

The heat was oppressive.

"What's latched? What are you talking about?"

"Something has…"

Her voice turned into a shrill whistle that hurt his ears.

"…like a spiritual lamprey, like a…"

Skree-ee!

The car lurched as he ran over a branch in the middle of the road. He felt it catch in the rear wheel well, could hear the leaves flapping against the tire.

The recording started up again.

Describe this grey man to me again…

GROWL.

"Mr. Larson? Are you still there?"

Sweat ran into his eyes, stinging them.

"I feel it's my duty to warn you…"

Skree-ee-ee!

Peter grabbed his phone and threw it into the back seat where Ellen continued to talk.

I can't see shit.

He rubbed at the windshield with his arm and only managed to erase a small window in the fogged glass.

A truck roared past, and the spray it kicked up was tremendous.

I've got to pull off at the next exit.

The pain in his stomach grew sharply more acute. He coughed, the taste of bile filling his mouth.

I'm going to lose my lunch.

"Don't you get sick in this car!"

Peter felt the world drop out from under him. He turned his head slowly to his right. Myrna Larson was sitting in the passenger seat just inches away.

The smell of her rot was appalling.

"I paid good money for that meal. You're insulting me, boy. You're *insulting* me!"

The woman spat her venom through yellowed and missing teeth. Her skin was blue, and her face hung limp. Her gnarled hands flapped about in her lap like injured birds, and suddenly she *was* a bird, her head transformed into that of a hideous, black crow with a gaping beak.

Skree! Skree-ee!

The dead woman with the bird's head snapped at him, and Peter swerved to the shoulder, skidding as he braked.

Skree!

The hooked beak bit at his face, drawing blood. His mother's arms became wings, which swatted and slapped him in their feathered fury. He heard bones snap as she beat him down.

Skree!

And then, she was gone.

"Mr. Larson?"

Peter looked at the dashboard. His hazards were on. The car was in park.

"What's going on?" Ellen asked from the back seat. "Hello?"

Peter turned off the hazard lights and threw the car into drive.

"Are you still there?"

To tell you the truth, I don't know anymore.

CHAPTER 29

As Peter plucked the remains of the branch from the wheel well, parked beneath the shelter of a truck stop canopy, he saw that the woman fueling up her SUV next to him was staring.

"You should put some antiseptic on that," she said, pointing to the wound on his face.

"Thanks. I will."

Images of his mother, his bird mother, flashed in his head. Dead eyes and hungry beak.

"What happened?"

Peter pulled back from the fog. "Huh?"

"To your face?" The woman seemed more concerned than curious, so Peter told her.

"I got pecked by a bird."

Pecked.

The word struck him as funny, and he stifled a laugh.

"They carry diseases, you know. That avian flu."

Peter Piper the pickled pepper picker picked a peck-peck-peck...

He giggled aloud this time. The woman was not amused. She quickly topped off her tank and got back into her SUV.

His phone rang. Ellen again. He'd told her he would call her back as soon as he got off the road. The gal was impatient.

"It's an entity, and that's outside of my area of expertise."

"Mine too, Ms. Marx."

160

"Are you being sarcastic? I don't understand sarcasm."

Peter steered her back on track. "An entity, you said?"

"Yes. Not a spirit; not a ghost. Ghosts live in loops. Like a song that plays over and over again. And that song is a recording of something that's been. That's haunting. This is different. This frankly scares me a lot."

The sky pulsed with lightning. "So, do I just throw out everything you told me to try—"

"No! The sonics, the prayers—those are good things. They might help confuse it. Confused is good. But they aren't going to solve your problem."

Peter switched ears. The gouge in his face was starting to hurt.

"I'm going to have to do some research. I'll miss tai chi tonight, but that's okay. Sometimes we have to make adjustments. It doesn't mean that everything gets thrown out of whack." This last bit was by rote as if she were parroting someone else's words. "We'll talk again soon." Once again, she was gone without fanfare.

The phone rang as he pulled away from the truck stop. Hannah. He let her call go to voicemail.

* * *

"At the sound of the tone, please leave your message," chirped the automated voicemail.

"Hey, all of downtown just lost power," Hannah said, lighting another candle. "I may need you to pick me up sooner than later. I'll buzz you back after the owner figures out what's what. Okay?"

161

The crowd had dwindled to two tables of locals, the college students having departed soon after the lights had. Riggs kept them occupied with jokes and free chips.

Pat Porter, the Blind Rock's owner, came in through the back door, a cane in one hand, a heavy-duty flashlight in the other.

"What's the good news, Pat?" Riggs called.

"That I get to fork out a couple thousand bucks on a new generator," the old man said.

The two tables responded by asking for their bill. Riggs tried to cajole them into staying, but the matriarch of the group said, "I got cold beer back home. And power."

Hannah took a towel over to where Pat stood wiping the rain from his eyes.

"Thanks, darlin'. You're the new gal, right? Peter Larson's wife."

"That's me."

"I knew that father of his. Bill. Did me a kindness or two back in the day. I heard about Myrna. That's tough."

"Yes, it is."

The old fellow hunched his shoulders. "I know I should go out and see the old buzzard, but I'm not so sure I could take it. Sometimes it's best to remember folks like they were." He clapped a hand on Hannah's shoulder in a fatherly gesture. "When you see him, tell him Pat Porter says hey."

"I'll do that, Mr. Porter."

The last of the patrons exited the front.

"Shuttin' it down, chief?" Riggs asked.

"Damn straight. Hold on a sec, Riggs." The man pulled a stack of laminated cards from his pocket. "Here are your passes for the Fall Festival. Make sure you give one to our beer distributor too."

"Thanks, boss. Will do."

"I'd like to hear more about your research sometime, Mr. Porter," Hannah said, reaching for her phone. "Riggs told me how you came up with the name for this place."

"Sometimes when you go digging you find some pretty horrible stuff. Why don't you two go ahead? I'll lock up."

Hannah dialed Peter. After a couple of rings, she gave up.

"Riggs," she said. "Think you could give me a ride?"

* * *

The rain pooled in puddles on the gravel drive up to the house. Lightning danced amongst the clouds.

"That'll be thirty-two dollars," Riggs said as he pulled the Jeep alongside the front door. "But I'm inclined to give you the friends and family discount."

The house was dark, and the Prius was nowhere to be seen.

"That's awfully kind of you," said Hannah.

Riggs leaned in close. "I'll settle for a buck fifty and a kiss."

Before Hannah knew what was happening, Riggs pressed his lips to hers. His hand went to her shoulder, drawing her in. The scent of patchouli was overwhelming.

Hannah shoved him against the door.

"What are you doing?"

"I thought—"

"What the hell?"

"I'm sorry, I—"

Now it was Hannah who leaned in. She jabbed a finger into his chest, hard enough that it made him wince.

"Not going to happen, Riggs."

"I get it."

She jabbed again.

"Are you sure?"

"Yes, yes! Believe me. I get it."

Hannah withdrew. "What the hell were you thinking?"

Riggs couldn't look her in the eye. "I've been so lonely, and then you came along and, Jeez, the way you danced on the bar," he blathered. "I thought we were getting on real well, like a real team."

"We were. We are. But don't ruin it."

"Okay."

"I'm married, Riggs."

"I know. I'm sorry. If you need to quit—"

"I'm not quitting. I like my job. But you've got to shut this down right now, understand?"

"I got it."

"Good."

They sat for a moment in silence, save for the tapping of Riggs' fingers on the steering wheel.

"You gotta admit," Riggs finally said, breaking the mood. "It was a pretty balls out move."

"Yeah. You couldn't have fucked up with more gusto if you tried."

The two broke into uncontrollable peals of laughter.

"I'm still mad at you," Hannah said between snorts. "You *cannot* pull that shit again."

"Aye aye, cap'n," Riggs said, offering her his best hangdog look. "You...you're not going to tell Peter, are you?"

Hannah looked back at the dark house. There was a light coming from the basement window well. No power outage here.

"No."

She opened the door.

"You going to be okay? I could wait, if you want me to," Riggs offered. She could tell he was eager to scram.

"I'll be fine. Go home and take a cold shower, boss."

Riggs gave her a little salute.

Hannah turned and walked briskly up the cracked sidewalk. Thunder echoed across the plains as she drew her key from her purse and unlocked the front door.

CHAPTER 30

Rain dripped from Hannah's hair as she stood in the foyer. She knew Peter wasn't here, but still, she called his name. No answer.

After kicking off her boots, she hung her jacket up on the coat tree Peter had found in the second upstairs bedroom—the smaller of the two. It had been a child's room, once upon a time; she was sure of it. There was no substantial evidence to back this up, but there were clues that only a parent would notice. The notches cut in the windowsill by a penknife; the pinholes in the wallpaper from posters tacked up, taken down, tacked up again.

Not a girl's room. A *boy's* room.

It was now the depository for all things Hannah. Her grandfather's record albums, boxes of cookbooks and the large wardrobe box containing the dresses that seemed so out of place here in Maple City.

She walked to the kitchen to make some coffee and then remembered—no pot. She'd dropped it when Peter grabbed her arm. She'd never seen him like that before. *Crazed* like that. Even in Michael's darkest days, Peter kept a steady hand on the wheel. But not *that* night. That night he was jackknifing all over the road.

Hannah opted for mint tea instead. The kettle had just started boiling when she thought she heard someone mumble just outside the room.

"Peter?"

She listened, but the only sound she heard was the kettle's gentle whistle.

"You left me high and dry, you know," she scolded. "Your phone better be broken, mister."

She poured hot water over the teabag; the scent of mint hit her nose.

"Peter?"

She turned off the stovetop and stepped into the hallway, the still steaming kettle gripped in her hand. If someone *was* there—and if that someone *wasn't* Peter—they were going to get a faceful of boiling water.

What if it's Riggs?

She tossed the idea aside. Riggs might be a horndog, but he wasn't stupid. Or dangerous.

"Is someone there?"

A door slammed, and Hannah dropped the kettle. Hot water splashed across a stockinged foot.

"Fuck, fuck, fuck!" She stripped off the wet sock and tossed it aside. The boiling water had already done its damage; a large, red oval welt was already forming on the top of her foot.

Hannah slipped off her other sock.

Determined not to let her nerves get the best of her, she marched toward the back of the house and quickly tested the door. Locked.

Did I lock the front?

She was about to check when she noticed that the basement door was standing wide open. And a light glowed from below.

Her first instinct was to dowse the light, shut the door and retire to the comfort and safety of the upstairs bedroom. Peter would return eventually—of that she had no doubt. They had both moved on so quickly after his mother's funeral, and even though he'd had a strained relationship with the woman, he couldn't be faulted for being off his game. Well, not completely. Moodiness was one thing—going AWOL was another.

She walked to the door, placed her hand on it and heard a sigh. Not the wind; not the house settling.

A child's sigh.

Instinct coaxed her forward, and soon she found herself halfway down the stairs. The wooden steps were cold beneath her bare feet. And as she made the conscious decision to continue downward, she felt a familiar ache rise—a combination of fear and comfort in coming when called. What would be behind the cry? A bad dream? A stomachache? An allergic reaction to treatment?

Michael had had all three. One night, he'd called out to her in a panic, screaming that the bed was on fire. The mercury in the thermometer said he had a fever of one-hundred and four degrees. A frantic cab ride later, the doctors were pumping him full of medicine and pushing fluids.

Peter had been quiet that trip. As if he knew what was coming. Two weeks later, they were picking out the outfit their son would be buried in.

She reached the bottom step and dared not go farther. Peter had yet to do a thorough cleaning, and she could imagine a minefield of rocks and rusted nails waiting to do her in.

Hannah looked to the left, into the depths of the basement and pulled back. But what at first glance had been a hulking figure emerging from the darkness proved to be nothing more than a stack of cardboard boxes.

She checked herself, glad that she hadn't screamed. But as she watched, the topmost box slid from its perch atop the cardboard tower and hit the floor in an explosion of papers.

All her senses shot to high alert.

Dozens of manila folders now lay spread across the floor; their contents fanned out like cards—like the darkness was offering up a magic trick.

Pick a card, any card.

Hannah stepped down. The cement was cold. Undeterred, she picked her way toward the spray of papers, and, kneeling, picked up a large, manila envelope and peeked inside. Receipts for car air fresheners.

She picked up a folder. It contained a legal pad covered in Peter's father's handwriting—questions about the possible purchase of a mini-golf course.

Hannah had just picked up a folder labeled *From the Law Offices of Moots and Perrin* when she heard a metal clank echo from upstairs. The kettle she'd left lying in the hallway—someone had just kicked it.

"Peter?"

The door at the top of the stairs opened, and Hannah heard the weighty creak of a step.

* * *

Peter urged the complaining Prius on, its engine gasping like an overworked horse. The Blind Rock had been dark, and he hadn't dared listen to Hannah's messages.

His face hurt like a bitch. He'd only glanced at the wound in the rearview mirror once, but that was enough to know that he'd have a scar where the black, glistening hole lay. It hadn't bled—not much. It was as if the gash had been cauterized.

Keeping his mind on his wound rather than on what had caused it had been his modus operandi during the sluggish trip home, but now that the house was close, his thoughts turned to the *thing*. But even now, his recollection of the event was fading. Was it his mother? A bird? Or something in between? The memory seemed to have wings of its own and was quickly escaping, leaving him with a blur of fear and an ache in his jaw.

As he turned down the drive, a Jeep flew past him heading away from the house. One of its headlights was out.

Was that Riggs behind the wheel?

The Prius choked, and Peter pumped the gas. It stuttered a bit, then roared back to life. As if a switch were suddenly flipped, the knocking and the wheezing from under the hood ceased.

Now, you cooperate.

Peter pulled up the drive and parked under the outstretched branches of a protective elm. He got out of the car and briefly considered hauling his new audio equipment into the house but decided to wait for the next break in the rain. He'd maxed out a card on the additional speakers and cables— no reason to risk soaking the stuff.

The light coming from the front windows told him that Hannah was home, and he girded himself for the barrage of questions he knew would be coming his way.

Where have you been? Why didn't you answer your phone? What the hell happened to your face?

He didn't have a story ready, but—banking on his ability to come up with one quickly enough—he opened the front door and stepped inside.

"Hannah?"

The pungent air that hit his nose nearly knocked him to his feet. It was sickly sweet, like fermented flesh. The scent set off alarm bells.

"Hannah!"

The upstairs was dark. The light was coming from the kitchen. As he took a step forward, a shockwave of sorrow struck him. It was a tangible thing, like heat from a fire. Tears welled at the corners of his eyes, and he thought of Juan—Juan who had never come back.

The hallway seemed to flicker as if there were a short in reality. And then the grey man stepped into the hall.

Quiet, you little shit!

Peter didn't hear the words so much as feel them. They were like cold fingers clawing at his skin.

Be quiet!

The grey man lurched toward the back of the house, and as he did, his foot struck something lying on the floor. A dull metal sound. The spirit—for that's what he was, wasn't he? A goddamned ghost?—cursed under his breath and lumbered onward.

171

As soon as the man disappeared around the corner, Peter made a dash for the hall. He made it as far as the kitchen before forcing himself to stop. On the floor before him lay the tea kettle he'd gotten Hannah a number of Mother's Days ago. And next to it, two discarded socks.

He heard the unoiled groan of the basement door as it opened.

"Peter?"

Hannah. She was downstairs.

Tossing worry aside—for what would hesitation serve should he find those ghostly fingers around Hannah's neck—he raced down the hall. When he reached the top of the stairs, he found the grey man already halfway down, belt in hand. The boy lay at the bottom of the stairs, the darkness gathering around him. A nightmare in duplicate.

But this time, Hannah was down there too.

"No!" he shouted.

As before, the grey man turned, and as he did so, Peter rushed him, trying to slip past and get to Hannah. To shield her from the madness.

But as he attempted to sidle past, an attraction drew him into the grey man, and then he *was* the grey man. Trapped beneath his rotting skin.

His thoughts warped and overlapped those of the dead man.

Time to do it. The little shit! Snap his neck, stop his breath. Easiest thing in the world. Then I'll sleep. Little shit. Little SHIT! Be rid of him. Just like his mother. Down he'll go. Into the drink. Down with her. Down, down, down!

Images flashed before Peter's mind's eye. The boy lying in a wet bed. The mocking face of an alarm clock. A woman with black, flowing hair and bulging eyes *screaming*. And he felt rage, old and bitter. A moldering anger that insisted he follow it down the stairs, insisted he raise the belt and strike.

He saw the boy cowering below and felt nothing but loathing.

Little shit. Mama's boy! Step. *I'll shut your mouth. Bind it tight.* Step. *C'mere and gets some.* Step. *C'mere!*

Peter tried to look away—he knew what came next—but his eyes were locked in place, his vision borrowed from the seething, snapping man on the steps. He watched as the blackness overtook the boy, flowed into him. Watched as the boy, newly invigorated, leaped to his feet and scrambled up the stairs. He felt his small arms wrap about his neck, felt the wood crack beneath them, the step becoming a trapdoor and—

"Peter!"

The grey man and the boy tumbled away. The room brightened with a sudden shock. Peter felt the chittering darkness recede into the shadows.

Hannah was on the steps below him.

"Jesus, Peter! What happened to your face?"

173

CHAPTER 31

Hannah held her questions until she had marched Peter to the upstairs bathroom where she cleaned and dressed his wound. After tending to the burn on her foot, she let loose.

"What is that?" she asked, indicating the gash that now lay beneath gauze and tape.

Peter's mouth moved, but he had yet to formulate an answer. "I…I'm not sure."

"Any deeper and we're talking stitches, Peter. What gives?"

He toyed with the idea of a fanciful tale—a run-in with an angry local and switchblade—and gave in to a version of the truth. "I really don't know."

Hannah sat on the edge of the tub and stared at him. He couldn't look her in the eye.

"I'm sure you know I had to get a ride. I'm sure you know I called—"

"Hannah, I'm sorry—"

"I know the funeral was hard on you, and I know…" She paused and nodded toward his face. "Did you do that to yourself?"

He felt the urge to grab at the lifeline she was throwing, to admit to self-mutilation while in the throes of grief, and yet, he thought otherwise.

"No. The car was acting up, and I must have…hell, I don't know."

"Were you drinking?"

"No."

"You swear?"

"I swear. Look, I haven't been sleeping well. We both know that." He finally mustered the courage to look her in the face. "Maybe I nodded off behind the wheel. It was raining so hard, and the car was acting up—"

"You fell asleep?"

"I must have hit my face on the dashboard."

Hannah's brow furrowed.

"You want me to give you a story that makes sense," Peter said. "But I can't. It doesn't make sense to me. Not at all." Finally, the truth.

Hannah folded her arms. "Maybe you need some help."

"Maybe."

"Maybe you haven't worked out all your feelings about Michael. And then, going to the funeral home—"

"You're right." He'd landed on his strategy late, but it seemed to be working. He would 'yes, dear' her into submission. Better that than to let her peek into the world in which he was now living—a world where the dead were restless and clawing. He would keep her out this, no matter what. And if he had to trade on his grief for his dead son in order to accomplish that, so be it.

"I'll look into someone for you to talk to," Hannah said.

"Okay."

"Maybe we can go together."

"Whatever you think is best. Why don't you go to bed? You look exhausted."

"I look exhausted?" Hannah said, throwing the roll of gauze at him. "Speak for yourself, husband."

"I need to go get my cables out of the car."

"Now?"

Peter rose and walked to the window. The rain had weakened into a drizzle.

"Yeah. You go to bed. I'll be up in a few minutes."

Without waiting for a response, Peter headed for the door.

"Peter?"

He stopped. "Yeah?"

"You're not lying to me, are you?"

She was barefooted and nervous and he wanted to tell her everything. But that wasn't his job right now. His job lay below where the cancer in the house resided.

"Never," he said.

* * *

After retrieving the bags of equipment from the car, Peter proceeded to the basement. The spark in the air, the whiff of the unnatural was gone. And even if it were to rise back up again, threatening to detonate his life, he would not allow it.

"I will not be run off by shadows," he said as he set the bags down next to the audio booth.

He pulled a fifty-foot spool of speaker wire from one of the bags and got down to work.

* * *

Two hours later, Hannah was awakened by a soft ping. The text message lit up the screen of her phone, and thus, the room. She rolled over and out of a dream.

"Peter?"

The bed was empty, save for her.

With a sigh, she reached for the phone and squinted at the message.

First Market Bank Fraud Alert: Card 6922. Did you purchase $759.96 Iowa City Electronics 30 Sept? Reply Y or N.

Iowa City. Not Galesburg. One hundred miles away. Not sixteen.

She set aside the phone without answering Y or N. She stared at the ceiling, wondering when, and if, her husband was coming to bed that night.

* * *

As Peter mounted his sixth speaker to the wooden beamed ceiling, he *knew* he was being watched, but he was undeterred. The watcher was curious—of that he was sure. And also amused. Although he had no physical sense of the thing in the basement—no cold rush of air, no half-glimpsed shadows in the corner of his eye—its presence was as sure as his own breath.

With his final bit of assembly complete, he slipped into the booth and fired up the laptop. He pulled out his tablet and navigated to the first of the links Ellen Marx's had sent him. *Removing Negative Entities, Energies and Thought Forms through Sound.* The website's predominant Halloweeny font didn't give him much confidence. He played the first clip.

A fluctuating harmony filled the booth, and he quickly lowered the volume. A couple of right clicks later, and he had downloaded the site's entire library.

He opened a new project file and laid down one of the clips as a separate track, then turned to Ellen Marx's ebook of prayers for the dead. The first was "Prayer for the Well-Being of Earthbound Spirits."

Screw that.

He flipped ahead and landed on "Two Prayers to Repel the Unclean and Unquiet."

Bingo.

As he launched into the text—overlapping the dissonant harmonics—he felt a new emotion in the room; a stirring different than the curiosity he'd sensed previously.

It was *hate*.

"Lord of All, I banish all foulness and relinquish my will to the light—"

The tablet's screen flickered.

Peter hit a key, and the playhead jumped back five seconds. He continued.

"I banish all foulness…"

CHAPTER 32

Hannah was not surprised to find Peter's side of the bed empty when she woke.

She found him asleep in his booth. The basement room had been transformed. Cables and wires snaked from the booth like malignant tendrils. Speakers adorned the rafters, surrounding the booth like a halo.

It looked like madness.

Hannah retreated, unwilling to wake him. Whatever this was, it had nothing to do with recording books. This was something gone haywire, and her husband was at the center of it.

I've got to get him out of this basement.

And yet, she didn't dare. To approach him felt…dangerous.

As she turned toward the stairs, her eyes lit once again upon the file folders and papers strewn about. She quickly gathered up the disarray, stuffing folders and envelopes into the boxes. She hauled the first of the two *Personal* boxes up to the car and then went back for the second. They were rich with the scent of mildew and dust.

Once the boxes were safely shut away in the trunk of the car, Hannah went to the kitchen and fortified herself with a swig of orange juice straight from the bottle. The acid burned her throat.

Peter's lie about his trip hung heavy with her, and it made her wonder what else he might be hiding. She realized that she had not been forthcoming about Riggs' attempt to kiss her the night before, but that was a lie of omission—a completely different animal. Or at least that's what she told herself.

The world felt unbalanced, like a spinning plate that might—just might—tip over and plunge to the ground if she didn't take things in hand. She'd call around, find a therapist for Peter to talk to. She'd go through the papers from the basement, see if she couldn't work up a deal with Lillian Dann to turn them from one-dollar renters into owners. Bring some stability to the landscape.

But first, she needed to get Peter out of the house. She had felt it when she saw him asleep in the booth, laid across his equipment with the speakers pumping otherworldly sounds through the basement. He was festering.

She checked her phone—she had to be at work in an hour. She scribbled a note for Peter on the back of a piece of junk mail and left it at the top of the basement stairs where he was sure to find it.

If he ever comes back up.

Hannah grabbed her purse and headed for the door.

*　*　*

The pain in Peter's face startled him from sleep. He flexed his jaw to try to mitigate his discomfort and only succeeded in making it worse.

His audio creation had stopped, the computer screen awash with swirls of color indicating the system had put itself to sleep.

His head pounded as if he had spent his evening pounding shots rather than recording tracks. There were twelve in all—finished audio blending what he thought were the most applicable prayers with the sonic clips he'd selected.

The darkness had departed around three in the morning. He didn't even question how he knew that fact, but fact it was. Either it waned with the approaching dawn, or his efforts did indeed have some impact. Especially track number four…

You're batshit crazy. You know that, right?

He extracted himself from the tiny room within a room—his joints cracking and popping—and looked about at his handiwork.

Batshit crazy.

He stank from his night in the booth. He was ready for a hot shower. What he was *not* ready for was Hannah. As he ascended the stairs, he felt like a rummy stumbling home after an all-night bender.

But Hannah had flown the coop, leaving a note to do the talking.

You need a break. Don't work today. I'll come home early if I can. Antibiotic cream in the bathroom. Love you, H.

Work? The idea hadn't even crossed his mind. He checked his phone to see if there was any follow-up from Ellen Marx. She'd said to sit tight—she'd get back to him. Zip, zero, nada. What he did find was a friendly email from Flatiron Audio. They were looking forward to getting back on schedule.

Peter's finger lingered over the email a moment before pressing the delete icon.

* * *

The whine of a power drill greeted Hannah as she entered the Blind Rock. A sturdy woman in work clothes looked up briefly, then returned to her work.

Pat Porter waved her over.

"That storm fried the electrics. I hoped Mattie would have them sorted by now, but it looks like we'll be dark again tonight. Shame. Thursday night of the Fall Festival always brings a crowd. Better luck next year, I suppose. I'll pay you for the day plus a little extra for tips. Not Riggs, though. That boy's got his hand in the till more often than not. Don't you, Riggs?"

Riggs, who was doing his best to hide behind the bar, gave his boss a nod.

"Sorry you had to waste your time coming in." He turned suddenly as sparks flew from the back of the room. "No, Mattie! Third pipe over, I told you that." The man stalked off, leaving her alone at the front door.

Hannah looked back to the bar. Riggs had grown a sudden fascination with the towel dispenser. She made a beeline for him.

"Guess we've got the day free," she said.

"Yeah," Riggs said, mimicking a smile. "I guess we do. I mean, you do. We both do. Separately."

"Don't think I've forgotten about last night."

"I'm sorry."

"You owe me."

"Sorry. I do?"

"Do you still have those passes for the Fall Festival?"

"You…want to go?"

Hannah shook her head. "I want you to take Peter."

The man literally gulped. "You want *me* to?"

"Yes."

"As a punishment?"

"As a favor."

"Okay."

"So, you'll do it?" She offered him a look that let him know he had no choice in the matter.

"Yeah, sure."

"When does it start?"

"I'm not sure." Riggs called out to Pat. "Pat, when does the fair open?"

"Noon," Pat said.

Riggs turned back to Hannah. "Opens at noon."

"Well," Hannah said, tapping her fingers on the bar. "What are you waiting for?"

Riggs grabbed his fleece jacket. "Heading out, boss!" He was out the door like a shot—a man on a mission.

Hannah walked over to where Mr. Porter was pointing out Mattie's missteps.

"Do you mind if I stick around?" Hannah asked. "Do some work at one of the booths?"

"Sure, if you don't mind our noise." He turned back to Mattie. "What are you trying to do? Burn the place to the ground?"

* * *

Peter winced as he applied the antibiotic cream. The wound was angry and hot. He discarded the old gauze which was oily

183

and stained black and replaced it with the biggest bandage in the kit.

He stared at himself in the mirror.

God. It looks like someone shot me in the face.

A pounding sound echoed from downstairs, and at first, Peter thought the whole cycle was starting up again. Only this time, the other world was growing bolder, attempting to break through in the middle of the day.

"Larson! Open up!"

Riggs?

Peter threw on a fresh shirt and went to answer his old friend's call.

"Jeez, buddy!" said Riggs as he opened the door. "Shave much?"

"Is everything okay?" Peter asked.

"My friend, it's more than okay." Riggs pulled two laminated passes from his pocket and waved them under Peter's nose. "Today, it's just you, me and that brain-frying, stomach-churning monstrosity they call Tilt-o-saurus!"

Peter put two and two together. "Hannah sent you?"

Riggs nodded. "Grab your coat. Boss's orders."

* * *

Hannah sat amongst piles of papers, the two cardboard boxes sitting opposite her in the booth. The collection was a treasure trove of Bill Larson's past. Rental agreements, auto purchases and sales, the occasional anniversary card. She even found a photo of Peter with his mother as she held newborn Gina in her arms. Gina had a sour look on her face even way back then.

The folder she was looking for, anything to do with the house—auction records, tax records, *any* records at all—eluded her.

She was about to call it a day when she found once again the envelope marked *From the Law Offices of Moots and Perrin.* An old document lay within.

Across the bar, Mattie's saw screamed as it cut into metal piping, but Hannah's world had gone silent as she stared at the pages in her hand.

"Mr. Porter?" she called. "Can you come here?"

Pat Porter obliged, joining her at the booth. "What can I do you for?"

She handed him the papers. "You said you knew Peter's father back in the day. Can you explain this?"

The man perused the pages one by one, giving away not a hint of reaction. Finally, he handed the document back to Hannah.

"I think you'd better talk to Big Bear about this."

CHAPTER 33

The Maple City Fall Parade, which ran the length of the downtown and marked the official opening of the festival, was not to commence for another couple of hours. Still, the carnival section of the fair was up and running—piped-in music played and the smell of fried food filled the air.

The fairgrounds took up about four square blocks of Wilson Park at the northeast edge of town, butting up against the woods on one side and open to the highway on the other. Fairgoers were encouraged to park across the street along a stretch of grass that ran the length of the old municipal airport.

Riggs ignored this suggestion.

"Best place to park is the access road in the woods behind the whole shebang," he bragged. "Learned about it when I dated a carny for a brief stint. She made funnel cakes. I must've gained ten pounds that fall."

Peter remained silent as they passed a group of chainsaw artists setting up shop, rolling out displays of bald eagles, bears and owls carved out of logs. He couldn't remember the last time he'd been to the festival, but the scent of hay and cooking pork assured him that part of him had not forgotten.

"Bit of a dip here," Riggs said.

The Jeep veered right and down an embankment. When it rose once more, the tires tried to catch hold of gravel.

"Hold on."

Riggs gunned the engine and the Jeep spat rocks. He steered the vehicle down a weed-choked path and came to a stop beneath a cluster of mulberry trees.

"Voilà! Our own private parking lot."

After cutting through a patch of brush, the two reached the open field behind the Zipper—a nasty derivation of the Ferris Wheel engineered to shake change loose from riders' pockets. It swooshed around with a diesel roar.

"C'mon!" Riggs yelled. "This way."

The ache in Peter's jaw had not abated. In fact, if anything, it was working its way into his molars. He spat on the hay-strewn ground as he walked, trying to rid himself of the sour taste building up in his mouth.

Riggs stopped in front of the Skee-Ball tent. "Let's start the day with an old favorite. My treat."

Peter indulged Riggs for three rounds, his opponent amassing handfuls of tickets which he traded in for a small mirror with a pot leaf printed on it.

"You eat yet?" Riggs said. "I'm famished."

Peter had to think about it. No, in fact, he hadn't had a bite all day. "What are you thinking?"

"You haven't *lived* until you've had a pork chop sandwich with waffle fries on top."

Riggs insisted on treating. He sat Peter down at a picnic bench and set off in search of food. When he returned, he had two heavy Styrofoam containers in hand. As Peter took his first bite of the sandwich, he had to admit it was pretty damn good.

"I used to save up all summer so I could blow it at the Fall Festival," Riggs said, slurping on his frozen apple cider slush. "This was back when they used to use real mice on the roulette table. Whichever colored hole the mouse escaped down, that was the winner. If you watched long enough, you could catch where the carny stuck the cheese. One day, I walked away with five stretched-out Pepsi bottles filled with colored water. Only made it home with three, though. What was your favorite game?"

Peter's headache grew twofold. Man, the guy could talk. When he didn't answer, Riggs looked him up and down.

"That chop not agreeing with you?"

"Pardon me?"

"Cuz you're looking a little green around the gills, Pete."

Peter looked down at his sandwich and realized he'd only taken the one bite. "I'm fine," he said. Still, suddenly feeling as bad as he apparently looked, he set the food down.

"I'm guessing you might not be in the mood for any loop-the-loops or spinning or shit." Riggs' eyes lit up. He grabbed Peter's sandwich and tossed it in the trash. "That's all right, my friend. I've got it covered. Follow me."

Riggs rose, shot two points with his sandwich wrapper and headed off down the fairway.

"C'mon!"

Peter had to quick step it to catch up, and by the time he did, he saw the object of Riggs' attention.

Up ahead loomed a semi-trailer adorned with a garish airbrushed facade in the shape of a mansion. A flickering sign above a large Plexiglas skull simply read *Haunted House*.

Peter caught his breath.

Riggs was taking him to the spook house.

* * *

188

Hannah punched the intercom button again.

"Hello? Hello. Could someone *please* open this door?"

A sickly buzz sounded, and she quickly pushed open the door. She stepped into Applegate's lobby—a score of elderly faces welcomed her along with the strong scent of bleach.

Ronnie, the young man who had taken issue with Peter on their first visit, had traded in his Star Wars t-shirt for a football jersey. He watched Hannah carefully as she headed down the hall toward Bill Larson's room, as if ready to intervene should she cause any trouble.

The nurse's station was empty, and she could hear a chorus of "Happy Birthday" coming from one of the rooms. She bypassed the desk and walked straight to Room 16.

Myrna's bed had been stripped and stood empty. No new roommate yet. Peter's father stood staring out the window at dumpsters where two orderlies were disposing of an old sofa.

"Papa Larson?" she whispered.

The old man turned. He was dressed nicely in a sweater vest and slacks, but the purple flip-flops did the outfit no favors. He held a picture frame in his hands, his thumbs worrying the glass.

"I miss her, you know?" Big Bear Larson said as if he and Hannah were already in mid-conversation. "So beautiful. You're sure she's gone?"

Hannah went to him and guided him to his chair. She took the picture frame from his hands. Its photo was missing.

"She is, Pop. I'm sorry, but she is."

Hannah put the frame on his dresser next to his case of cufflinks and a small, orange *Gideon's Bible*.

A look of recognition crossed the man's face, and he reached out and tapped her cheek with his long, cool fingers.

"Hannah Banana?"

"That's right. And I need to talk to you about something," she said in the most soothing voice she could manage. "Let me get you a coffee."

* * *

Riggs vaulted up the metal stairs leading to the scrawny ticket taker's perch.

"Shake a leg, brother," Riggs chortled.

Peter followed. Tinny howls and moans sounded from the loudspeaker positioned beneath the skull. With a pneumatic spurt, twin jets of steam burst from the skull's nostrils. It was enough to make one laugh—and he was. Not aloud, but a hidden caterwaul that threatened to break for the surface.

Riggs flashed dual fair passes. "VIPs."

The weary ticket taker waved them on.

"This is going to be so freakin' cool," Riggs promised. "You wanna go first?"

"You go," Peter said. "I'll follow."

A voice joined the ghostly music—a bad impression of the Count himself.

"*Velcome to the Haunted House. Enter...if you DARE.*"

Riggs elbowed him. "Dracula!"

"Let's go."

Riggs practically squealed and made a dive for the entrance. Thick, black curtains quickly swallowed him up.

Peter paused, listening to the tick-tick of a strobe light that wouldn't be effective until the sun went down. He could almost feel the electricity that powered the place rising through the platform, tickling the nerve endings in his feet.

"There a problem?" the ticket taker groaned, sounding like a part of the attraction himself.

"No."

Peter stepped forward. He parted the curtains, and a moment later he was bathed in black light.

* * *

Hannah held out the document for Bill Larson to see.

"Do you know what this is?"

The old fellow squinted. "My glasses…"

Hannah handed him the sheets of paper and launched a search for the glasses.

"In the drawer. The left one," Bill said. They were in the right.

Reading glasses in place, the man scanned the pages. As soon as he reached the last page, he went back to the first. Hannah put her hands over his.

"Do you know what this is, Pop?"

Bill eyed her and offered an answer he hoped was right. "It's Peter's?"

"I know. But can you tell me *what* it is?"

He brought the first page close to his face.

"Willa…"

"Yes?"

"Her name was Willa. She was so beautiful."

"Please, Pop."

Bill pulled off his glasses. His milky eyes had gone teary.

"You're sure she's gone?"

* * *

The darkness embraced Peter as he trod onward down the zigzag hallway.

Ahead, he caught glimpses of Riggs reacting to dummy vampires and zombies as they lurched forward, illuminated by artificial lightning. Each flash lit up the room, and Peter could clearly see the patched roof in those moments of clarity. Duct taped wires and hanging cords—a patchwork attempt at a nightmare.

"This place stinks. I love it!" Riggs howled. "Watch out. You gotta step hard on this rubber mat to get the skeleton to pop up."

A curtain made up of hanging strips of cloth loomed up before them looking for all the world like the end stage of a car wash.

"Banzai!" Riggs shouted and forged ahead.

Peter came up to the cage with the faulty trigger. There was a break in the soundtrack, and then the corny music started up again from the beginning.

He stomped on the mat, and the skeleton appeared. No fanfare—no shriek, no flashing light. He stomped again and again. Each time, the plastic collection of bones leaped up from its hiding place, but it wasn't until his final try that he got the full effect.

The faux skeleton jumped up accompanied by a woman's scream and pounding lights. The thing held there, quivering—its long, black wig hanging in tatters.

For all its flaws and artifice, it was one of the most frightening things Peter had ever seen in his life.

He fell backward—through the car wash curtain—and into the pitch black room beyond.

* * *

Hannah squeezed Big Bear's hand and girded herself for his answer.

"Pop, who was Willa?"

The big man shook his head, amazed he had to answer the question.

"Why, she was Peter's mama, of course."

Hannah's mouth went dry, and she took a sip of the coffee she had brought for her father-in-law.

She looked down at the first page of the document.

State of Illinois, Division of Vital Records. Certificate of Adoption.

CHAPTER 34

Peter's fall had knocked the wind out of him, and he lay on his back in the dark, struggling for air. Not that he could have risen right away—his world was spinning.

The canned wolf howls and thunder continued to play, but bit by bit they began to recede into the distance.

He staggered to his feet, catching himself lest he stumble. With no visual points of reference, he was having difficulty getting his bearings.

"Riggs?" he called.

No answer.

He thrust out his arms, hoping to come into contact with a wall or another person—anything. He walked what seemed like minutes into the void, and yet touched nothing but air.

As the soundtrack slipped away completely, a dim light faded up.

Peter found himself standing in the middle of a bare room. Blank walls all around.

He turned to look behind him. The curtain through which he'd fallen was gone. A trick of the funhouse, no doubt. The only way in and out of the room was a lone door set into the wall before him.

Go with it. All in good fun. The sooner you walk through that door, the sooner you're outta here.

Without another moment of hesitation, Peter walked to the door and turned the knob.

Locked.

He tried again, but the door resisted. Great. The funhouse had obviously broken down.

Peter was about to start shouting for the carny, for Riggs when he spied a latch positioned at the top of the door. He reached up, slid back the bolt and the door swung open.

Like the previous room, this next was also devoid of light. It was also small—he could feel the walls on either side of him. And as he tried to step forward, he ran into something standing in his path. He grabbed the object, and his hands recognized it for what it was. A chair.

My chair.

Little lights began to flicker before him—equipment booting up. He heard the familiar whir of a computer's fan powering up, and as the desk lamp flickered to life revealing his surroundings, Peter froze.

He was in his audio booth.

The door softly closed behind him. He tested the doorknob. Of course, it was locked.

Am I at the fair dreaming this booth or am I in this booth dreaming the fair?

A squeal of feedback cut his thoughts short, and he quickly adjusted the preamp's controls to silence it.

Whispers. I hear whispers.

Were they coming from within the booth or without? Peter couldn't tell. But as he placed the headphones on his ears, he got his answer.

Hushed and ragged, Peter couldn't even tell the sex of the whisperer until they finally moaned.

"Yes-ss-ss…"

It was Hannah.

"Oh, Riggs…"

It was his wife. And Riggs' name was on her lips.

Her sparse words were punctuated with little gasps that only a husband would recognize. And there was another here as well—lower and grunting—and when he spoke, it was with the suggestive chumminess of his old friend.

"C'mere, you. C'mere!"

Peter could hear the rustle of clothing as if the microphone recording the event were nestled down between the two ravenous lovers. The volume of their coupling grew in tandem with the pitch of his wife's screams.

He ripped off the headphones and tossed them aside. Gripping the doorknob tight, he turned with all his strength. The knob's stem bent, and the thing came away in his hand. He slipped his finger into the hole, desperate to trigger the locking mechanism, desperate to be rid of the building intensity of the infidelity.

As Peter struggled with the lock, he caught a whiff of smoke—a rank and oily smell. He felt the press of something slipping in behind him, crowding him.

Peter felt long nails drag across the top of his head, stroking his scalp in time with the heated moans. The lights on the audio equipment danced as a voice vibrated in his head.

Coming…

Pounding behind his eyes.

Coming…

Making his temples throb.

Coming...

Threatening to split him in two.

In!

He jammed his finger into the exposed lock and felt a sharp edge of the works slice into flesh. A spring gave way with a sharp click.

Laughter, hollow and chattering, the gleeful refrain of the insane, filled the booth. Peter shouldered the door, and it gave way with no resistance, sending him tumbling into the abyss.

* * *

Riggs waited patiently at the bottom of the stairs, drumming his fingers on the metal banister in time with the electronic version of "Danse Macabre" coming from the loudspeaker. The ticket taker looked on with annoyance.

A second later, Peter burst from the exit.

He didn't even try to match his feet to the steps; instead, he stumble-fell down the stairs and plowed into Riggs, the force knocking both of them to the ground. Keys, change and a cheap phone spilled from Riggs' pocket.

"The fuck...?" It was all Riggs could manage before landing.

In a shot, Peter was up. He straddled Riggs and delivered a powerful right to his jaw. Riggs felt something pop.

"Christ, Pete!" Riggs howled. "Get off!"

Peter struck again, this time with his left—a glancing blow that still managed to clip Riggs' nose and get the blood flowing.

"I know what you did!" Peter cried as he threw another right.

"The hell you talking about?"

The phone lying on ground lit up. The caller ID read *Hannah.*

"My wife!" Peter punctuated this with an elbow to the chest.

"Oh, God," Riggs wheezed, throwing up his hands. "I'm sorry."

"You admit it?"

"I'm sorry!"

The ticket taker and his fellow worker from the Scrambler caught Peter under the arms and lifted him squirming off the ground.

"Get security over here!" the ticket taker shouted to the crowd that had gathered, drawn by the commotion and the blood.

"No!" Riggs said, spitting red. "Not necessary."

"Hell with security. Call the cops," the Scrambler operator snarled.

Riggs stepped in and wrestled Peter from their grip. "Did he break your nose? No. Did he break mine? Maybe. But you don't see me crying about it, so mind your own fuckin' business, all right?"

Before the carnies could answer, Riggs quickly led Peter away from the haunted house, making a beeline for the snow cone stand.

* * *

The blue syrup trickled down the cone and onto Peter's hand as he sat buckled into the passenger seat.

Riggs pressed his snow cone to his upper lip as he drove. The whole middle of his face was turning deep purple.

"Go ahead. Yell at me. Cuss me out," Riggs said. He took the embankment at a good clip, rocks scraping the underbelly of the Jeep. "I'm an asshole. I deserve it. Don't just say nothin'. Saying nothin'? That's the worst."

Peter remained silent for the duration of the ride. He and Riggs both received calls from Hannah during the drive—both ignored them.

Clouds rolling in across the prairie made good on their threat to ruin the first day of the Fall Festival. By the time Riggs pulled down the gravel drive to the house, large raindrops were hitting the windshield.

Up ahead, Hannah sat in the idling Prius, lights on.

Riggs sniffed, snorting up a clot of blood and snot. "One thing you can say about ole Riggs. When he fucks up, he fucks up good."

CHAPTER 35

Peter waited in the Jeep until it was clear that Hannah wasn't going to be the first to leave her vehicle.

"Wait here," he said to Riggs.

"Good idea," Riggs replied, happy to comply.

Peter stepped out of the Jeep and walked toward the Prius. The rain was already collecting in the ruts in the drive.

The windows were fogged up—behind the haze sat Hannah. She didn't look his way until he knocked on the window. She rubbed away a circle of condensation and looked out at him, seemingly content to let him stand in the ever increasing rain.

Finally, she motioned him to the passenger side. Peter looked back to the Jeep and made a downward, jabbing motion with his finger. *Stay here.* Riggs nodded.

Peter circled the car, taking a quick glance at the house. It sat silent like a hulking audience of one. He could feel the eyes of every denizen of the dark watching him as he opened the passenger door and got into the car.

He looked down at his hands before looking at his wife. The knuckles on his right hand were alternately red and blue—blood and syrup.

The jealousy and hurt that simmered beneath the surface begged for his voice, but he stayed silent, determined to make her speak first. When she did, her words caught him off guard.

"When did you start keeping secrets from me?"

Peter looked up. Hannah had turned toward him, and he could tell that there wasn't a shred of artifice in her question.

"Me? That's funny. That's a laugh riot."

Hannah didn't respond. Instead, she searched his face. Her gaze had always unhinged and unmasked him—he'd learned early on in their marriage that he couldn't keep even the slightest untruth from her once she locked on. And it was this power she used on him now.

"I know what you did," he said, echoing his words to Riggs before fists flew and blood flowed. "With him." He thrust an accusatory finger in the direction of the Jeep.

Hannah shook her head. "What did he tell you?"

Nothing! He didn't have to tell me a goddamn thing. I heard you! Both of you!

"Enough," Peter said. "He told me enough."

She squeezed the bridge of her nose and sighed.

"Am I boring you?" he asked.

"Look at yourself, Peter." She flipped down the sun visor in front of him and slipped aside the panel covering the mirror. Peter saw his stubbled chin reflected there, an edge of the soaked bandage just in view. "Take a *hard* look."

He did. Peter adjusted the visor and found his eyes. One was twitching back at him; both were seething with fire.

"Yes. Riggs tried to kiss me," Hannah said. "But if you were in my shoes, would you tell the man you're looking at anything about it?"

"You did more than kiss."

"We did? Please, Peter, tell me all about it. What's your buddy saying? That he screwed me? That we got hot and heavy in that filthy Jeep of his? Did the nasty in the back seat with the empty beer cans and burger wrappers?"

"You—"

"Nothing happened!"

The force of the statement cracked his anger, splintering it. Confused but still energized, Peter pounded the dashboard with his fist.

"Yes, it did!"

"Enough!" Hannah said in a tone that brought an abrupt halt to the conversation. She reached into the back seat and pulled the document from her bag. "Here."

She dropped it in his lap, the discontinuity of the act throwing him.

"What is that?"

"Something you need to see."

Peter regarded the thing in his lap for a moment before picking it up. It crinkled in his hands.

State of Illinois, Division of Vital Records.

Peter was instantly aware of his heartbeat. The reflexive squeeze of muscle, the rush of blood. It pounded in his ears, each fleshy beat growing louder and farther apart until...

The cry of a baby grabbed his attention.

Peter suddenly realized that he was standing.

Not possible.

He looked left. Hannah was gone. The car was gone. Riggs, the pages he was holding, the rain—all gone.

The wail came again, and this time Peter turned toward the house. The sky was grey, the house in slightly less disrepair than a moment ago. And a green Ford pickup sat parked in the drive. Large swaths of the truck had been eaten away by rust.

The payload was filled with junk covered by a paint-spattered tarp.

Peter walked toward the house, passing the truck on the way. Glancing inside, he saw a ratty blanket covering even rattier cushions, and a half-empty bottle of Old Crow peeked out from under the seat.

When the cry came a third time, it was followed by a woman's scream. Peter ran for the front door and stopped, hand poised over the doorknob.

I could turn around—refuse to go inside.

Even as he thought this, the world stuttered and jumped, and he suddenly found himself standing inside the house at the top of the stairs. The instantaneous leap was disorienting, and Peter's brain had to take a second to catch up.

The two bedrooms stood before him. The door to the master was closed; the door to the second, wide open. Inside the smaller room sat a crib. Lying about the floor were cloth diapers—once neatly folded, now scattered.

A familiar scent caught him off guard, and he recoiled. It was the heavy musk of cheap cigars. The air practically dripped with it.

"You cheat!" The shout came from behind the door to the master bedroom. *"You filthy cheat!"* Peter heard the sound of an open-hand slap and a quick exhalation.

"Albert, stop!" A woman. Peter's guts trembled at the sound, whether in recognition of the voice or the fear that it contained. He wanted to run—either toward the woman or away—but his feet were glued to the floor.

The baby's cries kicked in again. A pathetic mewling—a sickly sound.

"Shut it up, or I'll shut it up for you."

Peter pressed his hand against the door, and it gave a warning creak. He pulled his hand back, not wanting to alert the people within the room of his presence.

He wanted to look inside, to *see* inside. There was no doubt in his mind that if he threw the door open, he would come face to face with the grey man—now named. *Albert.*

The woman began cooing, a gentle sound meant to soothe interrupted by hacking sobs. He could see the woman in his mind's eye, stroking the child's head, desperate to instill calm.

"Back in my old man's day, they had a name for women like you. Jezebel! Wonton women who spread their legs for any man who came sniffin' their way." He underlined this point with another slap. The woman's cooing only grew in volume.

"Go downstairs, Albert. I'm begging you." The plea was pure terror.

"That ain't begging. I'll show you begging. I know that child ain't mine—"

"Yes, he is!"

"Who'd you sleep with? You sleep with the Bear? Is that his cub?"

"No!"

"Man I work beside day in, day out. I hope he made you feel good, Willa."

"He's yours. I swear."

"I hope the Big Bear made you feel real good. 'Cause I'm gonna make you feel bad!"

Peter held his breath. *Big Bear? Jesus, it couldn't be.*

"I'll whup you so hard that ole Bill Larson'll feel it, by God!"

Peter could stand by no longer.

He threw open the door with a shout. The scene before him froze momentarily. The dark-haired woman in the nightgown with the blood on her lip. The open-mouthed baby in her arms. *Him* in her arms. The grey man red-faced and full of rage, lording over them both. A quick snapshot before, once again—like an old movie with a bad splice—the world jumped.

The man's hands were around her neck, and he was shaking her. The baby had fallen off of the bed and lay squalling on the floor.

"Beg me, Willa! Beg me!"

Peter shouted again, but the vision wouldn't hold still. The woman—*Willa, her name was Willa*—lay tangled in the bedclothes next to her infant.

The grey man—the Old Man—had his boot pressed against her throat.

"I...I..." The woman clawed at the man's leg and tried to speak, but this only seemed to encourage the man. He shoved down hard, and Peter heard cartilage crack.

Reality ripped once more, and the man was gone. Peter could hear him downstairs, cursing up and down and trashing the place. Finally, he heard the front door open, and the man stomp out.

Peter knelt before the woman. Her neck swelled, engorged, and he could only image what the force of the boot had done.

Her lips were moving in silent prayer, and with the man gone, the baby had gone silent as well.

The woman ran her thumb across her split lips. And as Peter heard the grey man reenter the house, the woman drew a bloody line across her baby's forehead.

"Shadow, I draw you forth—you dare not resist. This is your charge. I give my last blood to bind you. You must obey. This is your charge."

The air went cold, and Peter felt the bloody line burn across his own forehead.

The scene before him blurred. He felt time rush forward around him. The man was suddenly back. He yanked the woman from the bed and dragged her screaming across the floor, her arms outstretched for her baby.

Time leaped again, and Peter heard a crash on the stairs behind him. He rose to find the man glowering down at the broken remains of the banister, the woman entangled in its wooden teeth.

Peter stole a glance back at his infant self, but the baby was gone, swallowed up in shadow. The light was going out of this world, and Peter felt the panicked need to flee.

When he reached the top of the staircase, the man and woman were gone. A bloody trail descended the stairs and turned down the hallway, heading for the back of the house.

He took the stairs two, three at a time, feeling the house being eaten up around him. He dared not slow, dared not look behind him for fear he would be lost in the gaping maw that raged behind him.

Peter dashed down the hallway toward the back of the house. As he passed the kitchen, he caught a glimpse of Hannah and Riggs, naked and writhing on the linoleum floor. Jets of black flame shot from the top of the stove, engulfing the room in obsidian fire.

He ran on, outpacing the dark by mere inches until he hit the back door and burst into the yard.

Before him, the grey man held the woman aloft, wrapped in the truck's paint-stained tarp. He hurled the still squirming bundle into the pond. Dark water exploded into the air, reaching up for an even darker sky.

Peter couldn't contain himself—driven by instinct, he rushed toward the water. He shouldered past the grey man who startled at his presence.

"You little shit!"

Without hesitation, Peter dove into the pond—into the swirling, foaming darkness. Down he swam, through water as thick as blood, his lungs screaming for air. Reaching out with each stroke, his hands searching until finally…his fingertips touched cloth. He grabbed hold tight, digging his fingers into the tarp as his cocooned mother drew him down into the depths.

CHAPTER 36

"Get him out of there!"

Riggs plunged into the pond, quickly sinking up to his knees, and grabbed Peter around the waist. Peter's hand clutched a large clump of moss and muck, and for a moment Riggs was engaged in a tug of war. Finally, the moss ripped free, and Riggs dragged Peter from the murky water.

Lightning cracked overhead. Peter squinted against the thunder, but otherwise, his expression was blank. Dead.

"Why the hell did he jump in?" Riggs shouted.

Peter looked down at the edge of rotting fabric gripped in his hand. The bulk of the thing sat half in, half out of the water. And through a rip in the grimy cloth, Peter spied the toothy grin of a yellowed skull.

Willa.

"Is he breathing?" Hannah was frantic. She dropped to the ground next to Peter.

"Yes," Riggs said.

"Are you sure?"

"He's breathing. He's okay."

Hannah glared at Riggs. "He is *not* okay. Jesus Christ, look at him."

"I just meant—"

"What's that?"

"What's what?"

"That. In his hand."

"Just weeds." Riggs lied, prying open Peter's fingers. Lying, for he too had seen the gruesome, smiling skull.

"Help me get him in the car."

"Yours or—"

"Mine!"

The two of them lifted Peter from the muddy ground and hauled him back to the Prius. Hannah opened the back door and got in first.

"Careful."

Riggs maneuvered Peter in behind Hannah, making sure his legs were clear before slamming the door shut. He ran around the car and jumped into the driver's seat.

"Where are we going?" Riggs asked, wiping water from his face. "I'm thinking hospital. Right? The hospital?"

"Give me a second."

Hannah took Peter's face in her hands. He opened his eyes and stared—there was no spark.

Riggs turned the key in the ignition. "Damn. How do you know if this thing's on?"

"Riggs!" Hannah's voice kept his hand off the throttle. She leaned in and spoke straight into Peter's ear. "Wake up, Peter. You've got to wake up, honey. I love you. Now, just…wake up!"

A light at the end of the drive drew Riggs' attention. "You expecting company?"

Hannah felt Peter's jaw move, felt his breath against her neck. She pulled back. "What was that, sweetheart?"

"I had her."

"What, Peter?"

"The grey…" he whispered. "Grey man. I know. I know now."

"What man? Who are you talking about, Peter?"

Riggs reached back and tapped the back of the seat. "Guys?"

"He killed her."

"Guys?"

"Hush, now," Hannah said. She ran her fingers through his wet hair, all of her suspicion and resentment washed away with the rain. "Let's get you out of here. Don't talk. Jesus, Peter, I thought I lost you. Just hush."

Headlights lit up the interior of the car, which had the effect of rousing Peter even further from his stupor.

"What…what is that?" Peter rubbed his jaw.

"I tried to tell you," Riggs said.

The silhouette of a person appeared, framed in the passenger side window. A rapid series of knocks sounded, and before Riggs could reach over to roll down the window, the door opened and a rain-soaked person hopped into the car.

"It wasn't supposed to rain for another two hours," Ellen Marx said, wiping her glasses. "I need a new weather app. Mine was not accurate."

"Excuse me," said Riggs. "Who are you?"

Ellen pulled out her phone and typed out a quick memo. "I'll need to do some research—find the best one."

It was Hannah's turn. "Who the hell are you?"

"Ellen," Peter said, almost smiling. "What are you doing here?"

The young woman in black furrowed her brow. "I told you we'd talk again soon."

CHAPTER 37

Peter straightened up, hearing his back pop in the process. He felt like he'd been run over by a train.

"Hannah, this is Ellen Marx—Ellen, this is my wife."

"I read Saunder's book on malevolent forces," Ellen said, speaking to Peter and Peter alone. "But his conclusions are shaky, and his Catholic faith tends to inhibit him. Brodinger, on the other hand—"

"Cool your jets a sec," Peter said. "I need to bring my wife up to speed."

Riggs held a hand up. "Hospital? Yes or no?"

Peter waved him off. He looked Hannah in the eye. "I've got to tell you something."

"No shit," Hannah said, but there was no malice in—just an eagerness to understand. And he loved her for it.

As the storm ebbed and flowed, and the rain drummed on the rooftop, Peter made his confession to the people in the Prius. Every incident he could remember, every thought that had consumed him from the moment he'd stepped into the house not thirty feet away. The details he couldn't remember he worked around. He didn't shy away from a word of it, and by the time he had finished, he felt much more firmly grounded in the world.

It was Riggs who spoke first.

"Wait…you thought I poked your wife?"

Ellen was impatient, having heard most of this information before. "I have questions about this latest incident. How you answer will determine how I want to proceed."

Peter looked to Hannah for her reaction. She was silent, watchful. He turned back to Ellen. "How did you find me?"

"You gave me your address before our interview, of course," Ellen said, perturbed. "Are you sure you didn't hear anything the woman said when she marked the child? Anything?"

Peter took Hannah's hands in his. "You must think I'm nuts."

"Shut up."

"I just don't want you to think—"

"Peter," she said sternly. "I don't know what to think."

Riggs fidgeted. "Look, if you don't mind, I think I'm gonna head on home. I've got…stuff I've got to get done."

Ellen shoved her phone in Peter's face, an illustration of a demon hanging from a tree on the screen. "Does this look familiar?"

"Enough!" Hannah kicked the seat in front of her, jolting Ellen and silencing Riggs. "I need to talk to my husband. And since I don't know what the hell is going on, I need backup. Riggs, drive."

"Where are we—"

"Anywhere but here."

"Time out," Ellen cried. "I can't leave Kevin here."

"Kevin?" Hannah was at the end of her rope.

"My ride," Ellen said. "I don't drive."

Hannah shoved open her door and stepped into the pouring rain. She opened Ellen's door for her.

"You two follow us."

"Jeez," Riggs said to Peter. "She's starting to scare me. What was that you said about the haunted house at the fair?"

A flash of lightning illuminated Hannah and Ellen, the latter attempting to argue her way back into the car. Hannah was having none of it.

She jumped back into the front passenger seat and turned to Riggs.

"Take us to Oak Street."

"What about my Jeep?"

The glare Hannah gave Riggs shut him up, and he quickly steered the Prius down the drive.

* * *

Peter's parents' house was lit up. As they pulled up, Peter could see painters working overtime both upstairs and down. The college moved quickly.

Riggs checked the rearview mirror. "Are they still back there?" Another car pulled up behind him, answering his question.

"Shit," Hannah said. "Where else could we go?"

"Not my place," Riggs said. "It's smaller than this freakin' car of yours."

Peter reached over the seat and squeezed Hannah's shoulder.

"Go straight," he said.

* * *

The Intermission Motor Lodge had added a new neon vacancy/no vacancy sign since Peter had last seen it, complete with tragedy/comedy masks. Tragedy for no—comedy for yes.

Riggs pulled up next to the office, and Hannah dashed inside. The rain had dwindled but still fell steadily.

"They're reopening the bar out here," Riggs said, eyes on the dark windows of the small lounge section of the motel. "At least, that's what I hear."

Hannah was back. "Pull around back." Instead of getting back into the car, she hoofed it through the interior courtyard toward the back.

Riggs considered saying something and thought better of it. After looping around the building, he parked in the space in front of an open room. Hannah stood framed in the doorway, arms crossed.

"This should be fun," Riggs said under his breath.

* * *

The room connected by means of a double door to the adjoining room.

"I told the guy at the desk there were five of us," Hannah said, tossing the keys on the bed. "He gave me a deal." She set a bottle of whiskey on the desk. "And, for an extra thirty bucks, he gave me this."

Ellen stepped into the room. "Kevin wants to stay in the car."

"Fine," Hannah said. "Peter, come with me." She disappeared into the second room.

"What are we supposed to do?" Riggs moaned.

Peter picked up the whiskey and tossed it to Ellen.

"I don't drink," she said.

Peter nodded toward Riggs as he headed for the adjoining room. "He'll teach you."

Hannah was sitting on the bed waiting for him. "Close the door, please."

Peter did as he was asked.

"Sit."

He sat, noticing that their sides of the bed had switched for this conversation. Hannah was in charge—no doubt about it. Peter was prepared to do whatever she wanted, recant the whole thing if need be. But with her first words, he had to reassess his position.

"I thought I heard a boy," she said.

"Excuse me?"

"In the basement." She waited for him to press her on the statement, and when he didn't, she continued. "Last night. I was *so* mad at you, Peter. You left me stranded. You *lied* to me. I wasn't thinking straight, I know that. But..."

Peter wrestled with the impulse to jump in, to apologize for everything. For marrying her, for dragging her away from the city. For poisoning her whole life.

"No," Hannah said, staring at her hands as if they held the answer. "I heard a boy's voice in the basement. Just as sure as I hear my own." She was crying now. "I can't wrap my head around your story, Peter. I'm trying to. Maybe if you'd told me what was happening *while* it was happening...I don't know."

They both looked up as the sound of murmured voices bled through the adjoining door.

"This girl. How does she figure into this?"

"She's an expert," Peter said, trying to convince himself as much as her. "The only expert I knew to call, anyway. I thought if I could deal with this on my own, put an end to it, I could protect you. You've been through so goddamn much. I thought I owed you at least that."

Hannah put her arms around him, and now it was his turn to cry—to expose his confusion and fear and sorrow. To her. To Hannah.

"That's not how we do things, you big dope," she said, drawing him closer. "We don't do things alone. Not this—not Michael. None of it. You hear me?"

He did. As he sat there with Hannah—embracing and embraced—he felt the tiniest nudge of something so foreign he barely recognized it.

Hope.

CHAPTER 38

Ellen held an untouched glass of whiskey in her hand. Riggs was drinking straight from the bottle.

A gawky teenager with blue hair sat on one of the beds flipping through TV channels with the remote. Apparently, Kevin was no longer content to wait in the car.

Hannah approached Ellen.

"Peter seems to think that you can help us. What's next?"

"First, I need some time alone with Mr. Larson," Ellen said, setting down the whiskey. "Then, I'll need to assess the exact nature of this situation. Masterson outlines eight steps in order to—"

"Fine," Hannah said. "Why don't you take the other room?"

"I'll need my backpack."

"All right."

"It's in Kevin's car."

Hannah scowled. "Then I suggest you go get it."

* * *

Peter paced about the room in bare feet—his soaked socks draped across the heater. Ellen sat at the desk rummaging through her backpack.

"Your pacing is making me nervous," Ellen snapped.

"Sorry. It's not every day that I get to take part in an exorcism or intervention or whatever you want to call this."

Ellen looked up, annoyed. "This is just research. I'll find out what I can. If it helps you, good—if not, too bad." She dug deeper into the pack. "Where is it?"

An image snuck into Peter's head, and he tried to bat it away—the grey man glaring at him, *knowing* him.

And now Peter knew *him*.

Albert. Albert Carver. The name on his adoption papers.

"Here we go," Ellen said. She pulled a small prescription box from her backpack and proceeded to pop pills from their foil container like they were candy.

"What's that?"

"Methylphenidate."

"And that is…?"

Ellen let loose an exasperated sigh. "It's Ritalin, all right? I've found that high doses help me see things better. And before you ask, yes, by *things* I mean things of a spiritual nature. Do you have any more questions? Maybe you'd like to write them down." She downed another two pills and dry swallowed them like a pro.

He held up his hands. No questions.

"Now we wait," Ellen said. "Eight minutes tops."

Peter slipped into the bathroom while Ellen sat stoically awaiting the arrival of her buzz. He filled the sink with cold water, submerged his face and held his breath. Fourteen…fifteen…sixteen. When he rose, he grabbed a hand towel and wiped his face, careful not to rip the bandage free.

He looked in the mirror. The light above it blinked once.

Probably the storm. Probably a short.

Probably not.

His eyes were bloodshot. Not only were they red, but fine, spidery veins stood out in sharp relief. He hadn't shaved in days. Early on in their marriage, Peter had sworn to Hannah that he would never come to bed without ridding himself of his whiskers first, but that was a different Peter Larson.

He peeked back at Ellen Marx.

You might as well have picked her out of the phonebook for all you know about her.

True. But when you're drowning, do you really stop to check the pedigree of the lifeguard?

"It's kicking in!" Ellen bellowed from the other room. "We can start."

Peter found the woman standing in the middle of the room, snooping about as if she'd lost something.

"Everything okay?"

"Yeah, just gotta scoot this little one outta here."

"Little?"

"Shh!" Ellen hissed.

She elbowed past him on her way to the closet, making shooing motions with her hands.

"Okay," she said. "He's gone. I didn't want to scare him off, but I can't have him distracting me."

Peter scratched at his bandage. "I'm not asking a question. But I think I'd be safe to assume that there's something in this room."

"There was."

"Something connected to me."

Ellen snorted. "No. Not everything's about you, Mr. Larson," Ellen said. "This is an old motel. It'd be strange if it weren't at least a little active, don't you think?"

She was starting to get on his nerves.

Starting? No. She'd managed that the moment I met her.

"Is it all right if I sit?"

"Knock yourself out," Ellen said, turning her attention to the ceiling. "I've just got to tune out the euphoria."

The woman finally pulled up a chair and set it in front of him. It was her show now.

"I'm going to take your hand now," she said, obviously not happy with the prospect. "I want you to clear your mind. Whatever you might be feeling, turn that off as well."

Easy for you to say.

"And no talking."

"I didn't—"

"Easy for you to say. Jeez, you've got a loud brain."

Ellen swiftly gripped his right hand in hers and gave it a meaty squeeze.

"Unghh," she burbled. Her eyes lolled, and her mouth went slack. If Peter didn't know any better, he might have feared she was having a stroke.

He remained silent as Ellen spasmed, her hand kneading his.

"Zz-zzz…" she buzzed. "Z'anyone nee-ee…"

The faucet in the bathroom turned itself on. Peter heard it distinctly. And as Ellen rocked and moaned, he listened as the water reached the top of the sink and began dripping onto the tiled floor.

Ellen's breathing turned rapid. The huff-huff-huff rhythm of one destined to hyperventilate. Her eyes fixed on his. They had gone jet black.

The full-length mirror next to the dresser cracked, splintering from head to toe. The TV flickered on and off.

Ellen pulled back her hand. She glanced at the water pooling on the bathroom floor.

"No!" she said fiercely.

She rose from her chair and stalked over to the sink, sloshing through the standing water.

"No!"

She turned off the faucet and stepped back into the room.

"It's playing with me," she said, disgusted. "I hate games."

"It's here?"

"Of course it's here. You're here—it's here."

"But I thought…I thought it was in the basement."

"It is."

"Right now?"

"Of course."

Peter grimaced. "You've lost me."

Ellen scrunched up her face, the effort of translating thoughts into words apparent. "It doesn't understand concepts like *when* or *where*. It's not bound by time. *When* is always *now* to it—it exists in the past, present and future all at once."

Visions of *A Christmas Carol* popped into Peter's head. "So, it lives outside of time. I can wrap my mind around that. Isn't easy, but I can do it. But you said it's here with me, but it's also there at the house? How can that be?"

Ellen looked annoyed. "If I'm going to answer that, I'm going need a little taste."

She took a step forward, her eyes locked on his.

Peter felt suddenly exposed. "What are you doing?"

The woman rushed toward him, and for a second he thought she was going to strike him. Instead, she took his head in both of her hands and pressed her mouth over his. Peter felt her inhale abruptly—a reverse resuscitation.

She drew back and loosed a howl that rode upon his stolen breath.

The room was plunged into sudden darkness. The same must have occurred in the other room—someone was pounding at the door.

"Stop this," Peter said.

Ellen only howled.

"Stop!"

He felt the woman swoop in close, her mouth on his ear, and he tried to push her away. Strong fingers gripped the front of his shirt, digging into his collarbones, pulling him in.

No stopping. No, never. Not for Whisper. Not for Mr. Tell.

"Get off me!"

No stopping. No stopping, boy.

Peter shoved hard and broke free of the grasping hands.

The next moment, the door between the rooms burst open, wrenching its hinges loose.

The lights blinked on in the other room first. For a moment, Peter saw silhouetted figures clambering into the room, rushing toward him, and he was certain he was a dead man.

Then Hannah's arms were around his neck, and he heard Riggs say, "Damn, Pete. You clocked her?"

Peter looked. Ellen Marx lay sprawled on the floor. She was out cold.

CHAPTER 39

Hannah sent Kevin to the office for some coffee. Ellen had no interest in coffee or in talking. Once she came around, she shoved aside all attempts to tend to her and escaped to the bathroom.

"You or me?" Hannah asked.

Peter walked to the bathroom door and knocked. "Ellen?"

"Not yet."

"I'm worried about you—"

"Not yet!"

The young woman launched into a rapid-fire dialogue with herself. Peter pressed his ear to the door to try to catch her words, but her pace was too high and her volume too low. The schizophrenic conversation continued for a minute before the door opened slightly.

"Just you," Ellen insisted. "No one else."

Peter looked back to Hannah and slipped into the bathroom.

Ellen cowered under the sink, seemingly unaware of the pool of water in which she sat.

"Close the door."

Peter shut the door and sat on the toilet facing her.

"I need to be sure that you're okay," he said.

"Not okay. No." Ellen ran a trembling hand across her lips, and Peter recognized the two-fingered grip of an invisible cigarette.

"I'm sorry. I didn't mean to push you—"

"Not important," Ellen said, waving him off. "This thing— *your* thing—is bad. Fascinating but bad. Could easily fill three books. Maybe five." Even in the throes of near paralysis, the woman was still mapping out her next book series.

"My thing. Do you have any idea what it is?"

"It's a duality, of course. Can't teach a dog new tricks. Is that a proverb or an idiom? What's the difference between them anyway?"

"Ellen—"

"Don't interrupt me," she spat. "I'm processing."

"Can I get you some water?" Peter rose and made a move for the stack of wrapped plastic cups on the shelf.

"Not helpful!" Ellen complained.

"Ellen, please, stop." Peter's voice was firm but pleading, and it caught Ellen's attention. "I'm lost. And if you learned anything that could help me, I'm begging you—help me."

The strange woman on the Ritalin high shifted gears immediately. She straightened up.

"It's bound to you. By blood. But it doesn't want to be, you see? I don't have a clear picture of how it happened, but your mother—this Willa—had some freakin' gift."

"How so?"

"You can't control something this dark—you just can't. But she *did*. At least to some extent. And now it's acting up. Rebelling." She grabbed his wrist. "It's like something out a nightmare, Mr. Larson. I don't ever want to feel something like that again."

"I need to know what you found out when you...took a taste of it," Peter said, taking advantage of her momentary focus.

"Help me up. My ass is wet."

Peter lent her his arm, and the squat woman rose. She turned back to the sink, unwrapped a small, complimentary hand soap. "Here's your answer to how it can be here and there at the same time." She drew a soap X on the mirror. "This is the moment your mother bound the demon to you," she said. "From that moment until now, you two have been inseparable."

"But why haven't I felt—"

"Be quiet," Ellen said, roughly. "Lemme get through this." She drew a horizontal soap line from the X across the mirror. "This is your life after you two were bound. And *this*..." She curved the line up and backward in an arc until it dropped down and intersected the horizontal, creating what, to Peter, looked like a shoelace loop. She drew another X at the point of intersection. "This is the moment you came back to Maple City. You see? Past and present overlap. The man in the present, the boy in the past—the thing with you at both times. This junction is very potent for both you and it."

Peter shook his head. "This junction—"

"Jeez, I thought I was dumbing this down enough," Ellen spat. "Two lights in a single room are brighter than one. Two packets of sugar in a coffee are sweeter than one. Two—"

"Okay, okay," Peter said.

"This demon is stronger and more active because you've brought it into the same space at two different time periods."

Peter's throat was suddenly parched. He ripped the cellophane off of a plastic cup, filled it with water and downed it. "That doesn't explain my goddamn amnesia about my childhood. What happened to my memories, Ellen? Living as a boy in that house, doing what I did to…" Suddenly, the phrase came to Peter as easy as breathing. "To the Old Man? How could it steal them?"

"Because it's a mosquito."

"Is this you dumbing it down for me again? Because if it is—"

"No, not a mosquito, but still…yes," Ellen's mind was whirring. "It numbs you before stinging. No. It numbs you *after*. It's being kind. But a thing like it *can't* be kind, so it does the next best thing. Or the worst."

Her words were coming faster and faster, and Peter strained to keep up.

"They say biological forces blind a mother to the pain she experienced in childbirth so that she won't avoid getting pregnant again and have another baby. It's like that. But not really." Ellen pounded her forehead with the palm of her hand. "Your mother bound it to you—to protect you because she couldn't. But some of the things it's done have hurt you."

Like helping him kill the Old Man.

"And so, it numbs you to your pain."

"And since my early childhood was nothing but pain—"

"It took those memories away." She let out a deep sigh. "At least, that's my theory."

Peter let this sink in. "Which is why childhood doesn't kick in for me until I'm eight years old. Until I moved to Oak Street."

227

"Could be."

Peter pulled his hand free from Ellen's grip, which had tightened tremendously.

"What next, Ellen? How do I get rid of it?"

Ellen breathed deep. "By being strong and fighting back. The two of you are bound in blood. But I have to warn you—if you should manage to break that bond, there's no telling what it might do."

"Be strong? Fight back? That's all you've got?"

"That's all you need."

Peter pressed his knuckles against his eyes until his pulse pounded in the sockets. "Then I'm shit out of luck."

"What?" Ellen shook her head violently. "No. You and it? You've grown up together. It may have had the advantage of hiding in your blind spot, but that doesn't mean you don't *know* it."

"I don't understand."

"I have a brother. Growing up, he knew everything that annoyed me. Spilled milk, certain songs, the sound of him picking his teeth. He knew how to get to me. That's true of this thing—it knows how to get to you. Doesn't it?"

A flash of Myrna—now no longer Mom, only Myrna—with her crow's beak biting jumped into his head. A bastardization of his fears.

"Yes."

"That's a two-way street, Mr. Larson. You may not know it, but you know how to get to it too."

Ellen fanned the back of her shirt, trying to dry it out. He grabbed a towel from the rack and handed it to her.

"Yours won't be a physical battle."

"Oh, no?" Peter said, pointing to his face. "It's felt pretty damn physical to me."

"In the end, it will be a contest of will. And in that department, you've got a few things going for you."

"Such as…?"

"Love, for one. Your mother's—your wife's. Plus, you *belong* here in this world. It doesn't. And it knows that."

Peter raked his fingers through his hair. "Thanks for the pep talk, but isn't there something a little…I don't know…tangible you could suggest? Something from one of your books? Holy water, a cross, the Sorcerer's Stone? Anything?"

"The only tangible part of this whole thing was your mother's touch," Ellen said. She reached out and gently drew her finger across Peter's forehead with a tenderness that surprised him. "Still, you can confront it. Test it. Provoke it."

"To what end, Ellen? Seriously?"

"To knock it off guard. To give you the chance to improvise. The stories in those books of mine are someone else's. They can't help you. You're going to have to write your own."

"That's not very reassuring."

"It's the best I've got."

She dropped the towel, stepped on it and mopped the wet floor with her foot.

"How will I know if you're right?"

"Simple," Ellen said. "It'll leave."

"And if it doesn't?"

Ellen shrugged. "Let's just hope it does."

CHAPTER 40

As the drugs wore off, Ellen began to crash hard. Hannah offered her the second of the two rooms for the night.

"It's paid for, and there's no reason you and your friend have to drive all the way back home in the dark."

Ellen conferred with Kevin, and they both agreed it was for the best. "I have to open tomorrow, so we'll have to be on the road by dawn."

She pulled a book from her pack and handed it to Hannah. *Demonologist's Dream* by Derrick Masterson. "Give it a look-see but don't get tied to it. I hope I helped. My address is on the inside cover. Send it back when you're done with it."

"Thank you," Peter said.

Ellen nodded. "Come on, Kevin."

The thin kid snuck out after her with nothing but a nod, closing the adjoining door behind him.

Riggs swirled the last of the whiskey around in the bottle. He'd managed to polish off almost all of it.

"What's next on the list, kids?" he slurred.

Peter picked up the TV remote and tossed it to him. "For you? HBO and a nap."

Riggs screwed up his face. "You're going back there, aren't you?"

"Yes."

"I'm sorry, Pete. I'm sorry I tried to kiss your wife."

"I know."

Riggs turned to Hannah. "I'm sorry I tried to kiss you."

Hannah nudged the bottle. "Have another snort."

"You're so pretty."

"Riggs," said Peter.

"I mean it, Pete. She's so pretty. Too pretty for me. Prettier than…I don't know. I'm drunk. I'll shut up. I…where's that remote?"

"You put it in your pocket."

"Yeah, I did." Riggs sat on the bed and slouched forward. "Hey, what about my Jeep? It's still at your place."

"I'll swing it by tomorrow morning. Leave it parked right outside with the keys under the floor mat."

"You promise, Pete?"

"I promise."

Riggs nodded. "Good."

He switched on the TV to the Poker Channel, threw back another slug of whiskey and promptly fell back on the bed.

* * *

Peter flipped through Ellen's book as Hannah drove. After a few chapters, he tossed it into the back seat.

"That good?" Hannah asked.

"Seeing this crap in black and white makes it seem even crazier."

They rode in silence for awhile—past a stretch of auto dealers, The Dollar Spot and a shuttered video rental store whose sign still touted its going out of business sale.

They passed the salvage yard next, and then they were speeding down a county road. The last of the lightning lit up the horizon as they drew closer to the house.

"What's the plan, Mr. Larson?" Hannah asked.

"Not sure yet."

"But you're working on it?"

"I am."

* * *

The rain had stopped by the time Hannah pulled the Prius up to front of the house. In his haste, Riggs had left one of the doors to his Jeep open a crack, and the dome light was on. Peter rectified that.

Hannah joined him on the sidewalk, and they both looked up at the dark upper windows, the patchwork shingles, the gnarled trees that flanked the thing.

"I'm going in alone," Peter said.

"Like hell you are."

"Hannah—"

"Not going to happen, so shut up."

Peter turned to her. "This is my fight."

"If I don't go in, you don't go in. End of story."

Peter took her hand, squeezed it hard. She was here. Through all the shit they'd waded through together, she was still here.

"Wait here a sec," he said, letting go of her hand and heading off toward the side of the house.

"Aren't we going in?"

"There's something I need to do first."

* * *

As Peter approached the pond, he could see the pale overlay of the past. The man holding his mother aloft. The splash of the water. The struggle beneath the surface.

He knelt beside the matted clump of muck he'd dredged up from the depths during his fevered vision. The mound was no bigger than a dog. Spreading apart the rotten cloth, Peter peered down upon the remains of the mother he had only seen in a nightmarish vision. Willa, reduced to a pile of mossy bones. Sifting through the wreckage of the long-dead woman, Peter found what he was looking for. He ripped free a bit of wet tarp and carefully wrapped the item inside.

Something tangible, he thought.

When he returned to Hannah, there was an urgency in his step and a small bundle in his pocket.

CHAPTER 41

The first thing Peter noticed upon entering the house was the decided drop in temperature. But that was to be expected, no? Cold drafts, flickering lights—all part in parcel with a haunting. He could almost hear the canned music, the soundtrack of wails and moans. The Fall Festival haunted house come to life.

What he hadn't expected was the pain.

Two steps into the foyer, the nerve endings in his wounded cheek lit up, dropping him to his knees. The gash was on fire.

Hannah called to him, but he couldn't hear what she said— the pain blocked out everything around him.

Peter ripped the bandage from his cheek and touched the skin with tentative fingertips. The flesh was fever-hot.

"Peter!" Hannah's voice breaking through.

He gritted his teeth against the pain, trying to force it down, but the pulsing waves only intensified. It knew where to cut him—yes, by god—it knew.

Hannah put her hand on the back of his neck, and he threw it aside. Every inch of his skin sent signals to the nerves in his cheek, causing them to fire.

"Vodka!" he croaked, hoping Hannah would catch his meaning—hoping she would remember the giant bottle, a going away present from Hannah's folks, that was still packed away in a box in the kitchen. When she left his side and headed for the hallway, he knew she had caught his meaning.

His molars felt like they were about to pop out, leaving him with gaping, burning holes in his jaw. In his mind's eye, he saw a swirl of feathers, flapping insanely close to his face, threatening to blind him.

He ran his tongue along the inside of his cheek and felt a divot in the flesh. He probed at it with the tip of his tongue, and the hole widened.

Holy fuck.

He pressed his fingers against the outer side of the cheek— hot and wet with discharge—and felt the rough tickle of his tongue.

The hole went straight through.

He withdrew his tongue and was surprised to feel a pincered nip at his finger. As he ran his fingertips along the slick surface, he felt another bite.

Peter screamed as the beak pressed forward from inside his mouth, ripping his face. A rasping caw filled his ears as his wound gave birth to the bird.

It tumbled to the floor with a wet splat, seizing and flapping, staining the floor red.

Hannah returned with the bottle and stopped dead.

"Stay back!" Peter gurgled, his mouth full of blood.

He lurched to his feet. The thing on the floor clawed and bit—legs, wings and beak, all broken.

Peter raised a foot over its head and brought it down. He ground his heel into its skull and felt a satisfying crunch. The bird kicked. And as he continued grinding his shoe into the mess, the thing began to dissipate, and soon he was no longer crushing it underfoot. Its body turned insubstantial like smoke rising from a campfire.

Then it was gone.

Hannah quickly uncapped the vodka and handed it to Peter. He took a big swig, swishing it about in his mouth—feeling the burn but *not* feeling the divot. Search as he might, the hole in his cheek had vanished.

He raised the bottle over his face.

"I wouldn't," Hannah said.

He did it anyway. The burn was unbelievable. He kept pouring until the bottle was empty and his shirt soaked. He tossed the bottle aside.

"What was that, Peter?"

"My old friend letting me know he's here."

"We need to bandage that."

"Later," he said, gathering up his bundled tarp. "After I end this."

* * *

Picking his way down the creaking, wooden stairs, Hannah behind him, Peter felt the presence instantly. He had carried Ellen's promise with him into the basement—her assurance that confrontation would trigger something within that he could use. Give him some sort of advantage.

Right.

It was the touchy-feely advice of an ebook author, and now as he and Hannah stood at the bottom of the stairs, he had a sinking feeling that Ellen's promise was bunk. That he had delivered himself—and his wife—into the arms of the beast.

Too late now.

"Let's get to the booth."

He led the way, weaving around the scattered junk, gripping her hand tight, memories of his younger self racing through the dark basement flooding back.

My room. It's always been my room.

The air was electric here—static building up before the shock. Time to move fast.

He opened the door to the booth, and the breathless sounds of his last visit, the thumping groans from deep within the bowels of the nightmare funhouse insinuated their way into his consciousness. The betrayal that *it* had conjured, that *it* had wanted him to hear.

This was no place for Hannah. He should have insisted she stay behind, forced her to take the car and get as far away from him as possible. But there was no stopping his wife when she set her mind to a thing.

The door at the top of the stairs slammed shut, and Peter knew what he had to do.

"Peter?" Hannah stood nervously awaiting his instructions.

"Get in."

She slid past him into the crowded space.

"Sit."

Once she was set, Peter flipped on the power to his equipment. The lights blinked, and the monitor hummed.

"What do you want me to do?" Hannah asked.

Peter placed her hand over the mouse. "When I say go, I want you to right click once. You got it?"

"Yes."

"What are you going to do?"

"Right click."

"Once."

The skin on his neck tingled. It was now or never. Peter locked eyes with Hannah, and the connection gave him away.

"No," Hannah said.

Peter stepped back and closed the door. He reached up and slid the bolt into place, securing Hannah inside.

"Peter, no!"

She would be safe, locked away inside. Or so he hoped.

He raised a finger, making sure she could see him through the window. The gesture was firm and deliberate, and it calmed Hannah enough to watch and listen.

Peter smiled at her—his wife, his partner, his friend.

He dropped his finger.

"Go."

Hannah clicked the mouse.

A choir of overlapping prayers and electronic harmonies blasted from the speakers, the sound surrounding the booth, disturbing the basement's silence.

The attack was instantaneous.

CHAPTER 42

A black mass poured into the small room. Peter spun about just in time to duck one of its inky appendages. The thing swarmed about the rafters over his head, clawing its way around the room like an enormous bat.

Off!

The thing hissed and spat, pained by the sound of the prayers.

Off!

"Not a chance," Peter said.

The darkness rushed around the booth like a great white circling a shark tank. It didn't lash out, only raged about the room. But then, there wasn't blood in the water. Not yet.

Peter saw Hannah cowering, her feet up and planted against the door. Her lips were moving. She was either praying her loving head off or letting loose a barrage of expletives—knowing his wife, he bet it was the latter.

Off!

The swirling blackness howled, reaching out to swipe at the booth, pulling back in pain. Great shreds of the demon tore loose and floated behind it in the air like ashes escaping the flame. Peter took advantage of the moment to scurry out of the room and into the open expanse of the basement.

This better work. If not, I've abandoned Hannah to that thing.

For the first time in his life, Peter reached out to his mother. Not Myrna—not the beater of children and the curse of his father's life—but Willa. A woman who had used her last breath to summon a protector. A beast of the ether to keep the grey man, the Old Man at bay.

"Help me keep her safe."

He reached into his pocket and withdrew the wadded-up cloth.

"Hey!" he shouted through the door to the small room, and for a moment he almost succumbed to hysterical laughter, for what was he attempting to do? To get the attention of a specter, a wraith? As if it were a thing someone actually did in the world of the sane. Still, he persisted. "Hey, you shitbag!" A child's taunt, but perhaps that's what such a thing understood. At least, that's what he hoped.

The swirling blackness didn't react but continued its screaming laps around the booth, its movement causing the large box to sway. Peter feared the booth would soon topple, spilling his Hannah into the open mouth of the demon.

Peter quickly unwrapped the clothbound item, the dull white object within revealing itself—a short length of bleached bone. A fingertip.

Willa's fingertip.

Something tangible.

He had no charm, no incantation as his mother had, and so—as he dug the bone into his wound, coating it in blood—he let forth the first words that came into his head.

"Hush little baby don't say a word. Papa's gonna buy you a mocking bird."

One of Michael's favorites.

The commotion in the other room ceased at once. The darkness hung suspended in the air. Waiting.

Peter raised the bone before him, presenting it to the thing, red and wet.

"And if that mocking bird don't sing, Papa's gonna buy you a diamond ring."

He set the tip against his temple.

The black cloud dropped from the ceiling, filling in the doorframe, blocking the path between Peter and the booth.

"If that diamond ring don't shine, Papa's gonna buy you a five and dime."

Slowly, deliberately, Peter drew the bone across his forehead, painting a line in blood as Willa had so many years ago.

The darkness shrunk and solidified—no longer intangible. Its substance thickened. Peter could hear it crackle as it condensed, drawing itself into the crude shape of a man. And within its misshapen head, two eyes—dull and flat—opened wide and stared.

Peter completed the ritual and held out the bone once more.

"This is Willa's. You know I tell the truth. Her words bound us together. I rescind them. Do you hear?" His mind flashed to Ellen and her insistence that he would find the words, find the way to stand up and *demand* his release. And, by God, if he wasn't doing just that. "I fucking rescind them, do you hear me?"

The figure before him stood like a charcoal statue, fixed and unmoving. A man of ash and ice.

And then, its gash of a mouth opened as it let loose a crackling fire laugh.

I am Whisper!

It lurched forward, smoke rising with every step.

I am Mr. Tell.

Peter backed up. This wasn't right. No, not right at all.

I tell. Not you.

It reached its charred arms out toward him, its hands breaking into fingers, and then it was clutching him. He screamed as his skin burned and froze in its grip.

I tell. NOT YOU.

Before the thing placed its horrid mouth over his ear—its hollow breath cooling and warming his cheek—Peter whispered the final words of the song.

"And if that horse and cart fall down…"

The darkness finished it for him.

You'll still be the sweetest little baby in town.

CHAPTER 43

Peter felt his mind go black, felt every cell in his brain crystallize and crack, melting in a cold rush. Washing him clean of himself.

Hold on. Hold on or there'll be nothing left.

He reached out his mind, grasping at any shred of himself, his life that passed—a name, a date, the color of dawn on the horizon.

Hold...on!

The books of Narnia he'd read. His first kiss.

Hold...

Camping under the stars. The last time he'd let Myrna hit him.

On!

But none stuck. He was slipping away, and on all sides of him the frozen watchfulness of the thing—Mr. Tell, Whisper, whatever the hell it called itself—was *everywhere.* And it was laughing.

"Daddy."

The voice was distant but clear.

Michael. Dear God, yes! Michael!

"What's wrong, Daddy?"

I'm coming.

"Why are you crying?"

I'm coming.

"Daddy?"

Peter grabbed hold of the memory, and as he did so, he grabbed hold of his son.

The boy's bedroom solidified around him. He was back in their Manhattan apartment. Gone was the basement and its dark inhabitant. The memory of his son had drawn him to the boy's side.

"Ow. Too tight."

"I'm sorry."

"Story, story," the boy whispered as he wriggled out of the hug.

Peter looked down at his son, pillows all around him, the head of his hospital bed raised. Just as he had seen before. But unlike before, he knew that this time he was getting it right. This was an unclouded memory. And its sudden familiarity sent a chill through his soul.

"No."

"Please," Michael moaned.

Peter glanced up at the IV stand. It stood empty. Not so the morphine injection in his hand.

"No."

You listen. I tell.

"No!"

The boy's bruised eyelids fluttered. "A story."

Listen.

Michael's breathing came and went with torturous rapidity, attempting to outdistance the pain.

Peter had no choice. For the memory was alive now—no longer hidden in shadow. The truth the darkness had hidden from him. His truth. A demon's kindness.

Like an actor destined to play his part, Peter uncapped the syringe.

"All right, little guy. A story."

He heard the words and tried to disown them, but he was trapped within them. Locked in.

"Once upon a time, there was a boy named Michael."

He placed the needle against his son's broomstick thin arm and pressed. The boy didn't so much as whimper.

"He was a brave young lad—the bravest in the land. And one day, the King sent him off on a great quest."

His thumb hit the plunger, emptying the syringe of its contents.

"For the King wanted…the King…"

Peter dropped the hypodermic needle to the floor. Michael's eyes were open. Why were they open?

"Close your eyes, Michael."

"Daddy?" The word was quiet and slurred.

"Please. Close your eyes."

He placed his hand over Michael's face. Still warm. Still so warm.

Tears came, pouring hot down Peter's cheeks. It was time. No more crying. No more pain. His little boy had fought long enough, endured more than a child should. Time to let go.

Peter struggled against this final act, but he was not in control. Not anymore.

The boy's lips parted in a morphine smile. *"Please, Daddy."*

His hands clasped a pillow, placed it over those beautiful, trusting eyes and pressed down, covering the boy with both pillow and his body. And he held there, Michael barely moving under his weight.

When he lifted the pillow, when the boy was gone, he would rise, open the window and reach out to feel the snow light upon his hands. He would call Hannah at her parents', but would tell her only that she should come. He would sit at Michael's side and wait for her to arrive.

Then the old trickster would do its thing. The blackness—his blackness—would envelop him, smother him, erase him. And when he woke, he would be reborn to his son's death. That was the kindness of the demon. To obfuscate. To obliterate. But *that* was the past.

For now, hunkered deep inside himself, Peter knew. At long last, he finally knew.

The thing chuckled in Peter's ear—a hot, gravelly sound that tore at his raw heart.

Be still. Whisper must obey.

Laughing even as it soothed.

He was nothing now, and he hung weightless in the thrall of the darkness. Peter Larson was gone, replaced by searing pain and sorrow. You could call it a mercy or call it love, but he had smothered his boy. He had killed his only son.

Be quiet. Mr. Tell is here. Time to un-tell. Shhh.

An anesthetic calm swept over him, dulling the ache. He longed to roll in its waves, to absolve himself in its numbing surge. But his thoughts caught on words whispered not by the darkness but by the light.

"Please, Daddy."

Michael's final plea. Had the boy been begging for release or to be saved? The lack of an answer ripped Peter in two. It was a father's duty to protect, and he had failed.

And now once more, the demon wanted to steal his grief.

"This is my pain. You can't take it from me. You have no right."

Shhh.

"It's mine, not yours! Who the hell are you to rob me of my pain?"

S-s-secrets...

"Enough secrets! If you take it from me, you will harm me a hundred times more than if I keep it, you hear? You're my protector? Ha! Then *protect me!* Leave me my pain!"

A weight lifted from his chest, and Peter suddenly realized he could sense himself again. Not just his thoughts but his body.

The thing's laughter turned cold.

Want it? Have it.

With that, it released him—mind, memory, fear, anguish all intact.

Have it all.

Peter tumbled out of its grip to the cold, basement floor.

CHAPTER 44

Peter coughed, dust thick in his throat. He was back. Michael was dead. And he had killed him.

As he rose, he felt something brush past him, almost knocking him off balance. Something—or someone.

Straining his eyes, Peter could make out a small shape rushing past, and he knew he had just been pushed aside by his younger self—the boy trapped in the never-ending loop. His childhood haunting him once more.

The boy pulled the door to the small room shut behind him.

You. Him. My boys.

The demon hummed, self-satisfied, and at first, Peter couldn't locate the thing. Finally, he spotted it clinging once more to the ceiling, a fetid, pulsating mass.

His cheek burned as did his forehead. Stupid of him to confront it so blindly. Whatever skills his mother may have had, they hadn't been passed to him.

The darkness pulled itself across the rafters, sounding like a wet tarp being dragged across wood. It slid down the wall next to the door, reached out a black hand and jiggled the doorknob, quivering with laughter.

"Leave the boy alone," Peter said. He took a step forward. He had nothing to offer the fight, but still, he stepped forward.

The demon turned its dull eyes back at him.

Not him. HER.

Peter froze. He had been thinking only of the boy. But he wasn't the only one hiding in the small room.

Hannah. Hannah was in there too.

I told you. About the needle. About the pillow.

No.

Told you. Why not her?

Hannah must never know. It would destroy her.

The black cloud loosed great claws and scratched at the closed door.

Maybe I'll whisper. Maybe I'll tell!

No!

Coming...

"Please don't," Peter begged.

Coming...

"No."

Coming...

"No!"

In.

It shoved the door open, and for a moment, Peter saw both boy and booth. His whole life in a snapshot, compressed into a single moment.

"Come on in, then!" the boy shouted. "Come in, come in, come in!"

The thing flowed into the room. The sound from the speakers stuttered as the world tried to decide *when* it was—present or past. The result was a staccato rhythm, the sonic tones and his praying voice phasing in and out. And without their constant pressure, the darkness was free.

It latched onto the side of the booth, arms solidifying, climbing up to the top. Dark nails dug at the seams, prying the panels apart and popping screws.

He heard Hannah scream.

"Get away from her!"

His heart pounded in his chest—one beat in the *now*, the next in the *then*. The crack in reality splitting him as well, driving him to his knees.

Mr. Tell! Mr. Tell! Mr. Tell! Mr. Tell!

And then, a thought struck Peter. Perhaps the world wasn't strobing after all. Maybe it was him.

What was it Ellen had said? That the thing lived unconstrained by time—the concepts of *past* and *present* having no meaning? Then perhaps when it had brought him back from his memory of Michael, it had deposited him here— in a space where both past and present existed at once, both fighting for dominance.

The X where *then* and *now* intersected.

Ellen. Annoying, crackpot Ellen and her soap diagram.

As the demon clawed at the booth—cracking it open, eager to pour his secret into Hannah's ears—Peter saw a pair of small, bare feet appear before him, and he quickly looked up.

His seven-year-old self stood in front of him, his eyes wild. The boy had escaped the room and was ready to bolt for the stairs.

Peter would escape with the child. Into the *then*. Into the past.

To undo what had been done.

"Hannah!" he cried. His voice caught her attention, and she stared at him, hands pressed up against the glass. "Don't worry. Everything's going to be okay."

And then, he grabbed hold of the boy's wrist and closed his eyes, and took a step back.

The quavering tones disappeared. The booth vanished as well. Hannah and the rest of the present gone in an instant.

The demon howled.

"You're hurting my arm," his younger self said, echoing his son's plea.

"Sorry." Peter loosened his grip but didn't let go. "It's Pete, right?"

The child stared at him fearfully. Peter got a whiff of the urine that dampened the boy's rocket ship PJs and realized that he'd have to gain the kid's trust quickly before he lost him to hysteria.

"Listen, Pete. I'm here to help. I know you're scared—I'm scared too. But I'll let you in on a little secret—that thing in the room? It can't hurt you."

"No?"

"It can frighten you. Hell, it *will* frighten you. But if you stick close to me, you're going to be A-OK, you hear?"

The boy nodded vigorously, eager to be convinced that he wasn't about to be chewed up and swallowed by a monster.

"Remember—it can't hurt you."

At that moment, the door at the top of the stairs flew open, and Peter's heart sank as he heard the voice of one that *could* hurt the boy. *Had* hurt him.

"I warned you, didn't I? I need my shuteye. Didn't I warn you, you little shit?"

251

The grey man. The Old Man. Albert Carver. Ready to do damage. Ready to flay the kid alive.

Shit.

The Old Man took a step down the stairs. "Be quiet, I told you," he snarled, snapping his belt. "But you don't never listen."

Movement caught Peter's eye, and he saw the blackness sliding coolly out of the small room. No longer fuming, it had suddenly gone silent as if relishing the situation, savoring in the Old Man's arrival and eager to watch the scene unfold.

Peter and the boy were trapped.

The child tugged at his arm. "What do we do?" Peter's hesitation only added fuel to the fire. "What do we do!"

Peter heard the demon's voice in the back of his head and knew that the boy heard it too.

Man will hit. Man will hurt.

"Shut up!" Peter shouted.

Stop him, boy. Stop him good.

The boy stepped forward—Peter yanked him back.

"Don't listen to it!"

But the boy was already half gone, already locked in on his course up the stairs. Peter felt the darkness encroaching. He sensed the magnetic pull it had over the boy, heard its promises to help him shut the Old Man down before he struck. To strike *first*. To end him.

The swirling shadow wrapped itself around the boy like a cloak, marching him forward toward the foot of the stairs. The Old Man responded in kind, taking another step down, cracking the belt—figures in a mechanical clock that was about to toll midnight.

As Peter crouched, helpless to stop the boy's progress, a notion struck him that was so simple and pure that he laughed.

The thing heard him. He knew this because the boy's steps faltered.

The Old Man continued his descent. "Thinkin' maybe its time for you to go. Let me sleep. Leave me be."

Peter laughed again, and this time there were tears in his eyes. For watching the dark thing lure the boy toward his fate, urging him on to the act that would seal his doom and seal their bond, Peter knew that he could finally do what he had failed to do before.

He could save the boy.

Not Michael, not his son. But the boy before him.

Rising, he brushed himself off. "Hey! Old Man!"

The man on the stairs paused and turned toward him. "Who's there?"

"I'd watch your step if I were you."

Albert Carver looked down, and Peter knew that he'd caught his meaning. The cracked wood of the third step down—the Old Man was stepping over it.

The darkness screamed. It shoved the boy forward, forcing him up the stairs, lifting him high above the Old Man and bringing him down hard.

The man caught the child, terrified of the furious shadow rising before him and enraged by the boy's assault. He attempted a dual cure by flinging the boy into the swirling mass while letting loose a ferocious cry.

The child passed through the thing like a stone through water, bouncing off the bottom step with a crack before rolling end over end across the cement floor.

The black demon retreated to the boy's side, shaking him in its attempt to rouse him. It shrieked as it poured its all into him, feeding him its strength, summoning him to rise and get on with the deed. All must be as it always had been! The act must be completed!

Peter made sure it wasn't.

"Hey, asshole," he said, taunting the seething man on the stairs. "Why don't you pick on someone your own size?"

Peter rushed the stairs, taking them two at a time. The Old Man was caught off guard for a split second but quickly recovered. His face reddened, and he whipped his belt toward Peter's head, the buckle catching him in his wounded cheek.

Peter responded by grabbing hold of the leather strap and yanking it from the man's hands. He tackled the Old Man, knocking him backward on the stairs, and when the man struck the shattered step, it gave way underneath him. His ass sank into the gaping hole, lodging him there.

There was a mighty rush of wind behind him, and then Peter felt the boy's fingers digging into his cheek. He didn't try to turn or throw him off—this was the demon's doing. The boy was its puppet. His mind was not his own.

Peter, on the other hand, was in full control. He looped the belt around the Old Man's neck and pulled. A debt was owed, and this man's death was the payment. But not at the boy's hand. He would spare the child that stain. The Old Man's death was on *him*.

The man was wiry and strong, and he fought back with a madman's fury, but with every thrust of his fists, he sank even deeper between the steps.

"You shit! You damn shit!"

"Yeah," Peter said. "You got that right."

With the boy's nails clawing at his eyes and the Old Man punching at his groin, Peter gripped the belt in both hands and let his weight fall back.

There was a snap as the Old Man's neck gave way, and a cry as the boy awoke, realizing that he was falling.

The belt slipped from Peter's grip, the friction burning his hands. He twisted as he fell, trying to keep from landing on the boy, managing to spare him only partially. It was his time to snap as he felt his forearm crack beneath him. The boy squealed as they fell in a tumble, coming to a stop at the bottom of the stairs.

Peter breathed heavily. He eased himself to the side, relieving the boy of his weight and sending shockwaves of pain up his injured arm.

No matter.

He rolled his head back, taking in the upside-down view of the basement. The swirling mass was poised and angry, ready to pounce.

Peter shook the boy with his good arm.

"Hey!"

The child gazed at him, and Peter finally saw himself in the boy. Not just his features, but his fear. He had to get him moving.

"Go!" he yelled and shoved the boy with all the strength he had left.

The blackness struck, crushing him in its oppressive grasp. Peter laughed as it swarmed inside him, for he had broken the rules, changed the past and broken the loop.

"I guess we're meant to stay together." The demon heard the thought—for now it was *its* thought as well—and was terrified. The darkness flowed into Peter as he flowed into it—both of them possessing each other. Peter devoured all its black intent, leaving none for the boy. He felt the severing of Willa's bond. The child was released. He would grow up unfettered, untouched. The boy would live and thrive—free from the demon, free from the darkness. Free to follow his own path.

And the price was Peter Larson's doom.

The demon's nightmarish mind merged with Peter's own, and they solidified, becoming something new. An insane coupling.

As the night folded in on them, sweeping them into shadow, they screamed in tortured oneness.

"We're messy! We're messy! I'M MESSY!"

CHAPTER 45

The boy waited at the bottom of the stairs, staring up at the Old Man wedged in the steps. Not daring to pick his way past him lest he leap back to life.

He stayed there all day as his thirst and his hunger grew. He remained seated on the cold floor through the night, eyes locked on the body. Watching intently, willing the man to stay still.

It was the next morning when he heard the call from upstairs.

"Albert, where the hell are you? Boss is pure-D pissed you played hooky yesterday. Albert? Albert!"

An oversized shadow appeared at the top of the stairs, and with it, the burly man who cast it.

"Jesus," the man said as he took his first tentative step down the stairs. "Jesus."

The boy could see that the man was wearing the same clothes that the Old Man wore to work—one-piece coveralls with the decal over the left chest pocket that read *Maple City Sanitation.* The man hovered over the gruesome scene before noticing his presence.

"You," the man called. "Can you stand?"

The boy rose, legs quaking.

The man weaved past the Old Man's body as he descended the stairs. He walked up to the boy, towering over him a moment before kneeling. He placed his enormous hand on the boy's shoulder.

"Look at you. You're her spitting image."

The boy spelled out the name monogrammed on the man's chest and wondered at its meaning. *Big Bear.*

"Close your eyes, son."

The man took the boy in his arms, hugging him close before picking him up and heading for the stairs. The boy felt as if he were floating above the world—up over the broken man, the broken step.

Bill Larson paused and turned back. With his free hand, he loosened the belt around the Old Man's neck and pulled it free.

"The man slipped, is all. The man slipped."

The boy didn't open his eyes again until he smelled the sweet scent of soybeans rising from the fields and felt the warmth of the sun on his face.

CHAPTER 46

Peter smelled the town before he saw it—a rich, meaty musk that had always reminded him of Purina Dog Chow. Later in life, he would learn that it was the smell of burning skin and hair as workers blasted the pig carcasses with gas-guns. The Primeland pork processing plant employed a large number of Maple City residents. And saw thousands of hogs to their deaths.

He passed the sign stating *Welcome to Maple City! Home of...* and that was it. The rest of the greeting had been painted out.

His phone jingled, and he hit the speaker.

"What's up, beautiful?"

"Vacancy sign to your left," Hannah said, country radio in the background.

"Roger that."

Peter flipped his blinker and turned into the parking lot of the Intermission Motor Lodge. The place was open for business but was still under construction. The windows to the attached restaurant were papered over.

There used to be a large cow on top of the roof of the restaurant. A black Angus.

He parked, taking up three spots with the Ryder truck and peeked in the rearview mirror to see the Prius zip in behind him. Before he had a chance to get out of the cab, Hannah scurried up to the truck and opened his door.

"Do you have the good card?" she asked, dancing from foot to foot.

Peter searched through his wallet and pulled out a fresh credit card. "Hold on a sec." He fished a pen from his pocket and scribbled his name on the back. Hannah grabbed it from his hands. "You sure you don't want me to go?"

"I'm a better negotiator. We both know that. Besides, I have got to *pee.*" His wife made a dash for the front office, the wind whipping her hair as she went.

Peter hopped out of the truck and into a puddle of water. Ah, Illinois in autumn—a grey, raining mess. A muddy splatter coated the sides of the truck. He'd have to run it by the carwash before returning it. Hannah was of the mind that rental vehicles could be returned as grimy as all get out, but his father had raised him otherwise. Rent a car—return it clean. Maybe that was because he had once owned a carwash, or maybe it was just that Bill Larson was a stand-up guy.

As he approached the Prius, he discovered he'd be pulling double-duty with the soap and water. The car was all mud from front to back.

He glanced over at the office where he could see Hannah in the midst of negotiations through the window. If she couldn't get them a cut rate for the next few days while they sorted everything out, no one could.

The call from Gina about their father's failing health had come not long after Hannah had first mentioned the idea of getting out of the city. Uprooting would be a bitch, but something about the way the stars had aligned told them both it was time to make the leap.

Peter walked to the passenger side door and knocked on the window, which lowered instantly.

"I'm going to need to see your license and registration," he said in his best cop voice.

Michael giggled. "I don't have any."

"Well, in that case, do you mind if I get in? It's a bit chilly out here."

Peter slipped into the back seat.

"You know, I think this is the first time I've ever sat back here."

"I like the front," Michael said, pulling his blanket closer around him. "You can see better."

"Oh, yeah?"

He tugged on the brim of Michael's new Cubs hat. If the boy was going to live in Illinois, he'd make sure he was a Cubbies fan.

Last winter had been hard on the boy. His prognosis had soured and the pain from his cancer had increased, and Peter had resolved to give his son peace if necessary. He had even gone so far as hoarding an extra dose of morphine.

When the day came that Michael's agony was unbearable, he sent Hannah on a trip across the Hudson to her family and gathered the needle and bottle.

But when he stepped into Michael's room, he paused. His mind flitted back to that moment in the basement when he'd thought all was lost. When the shadows were closing in, there had come a man who fought them back—a spark of light in the darkness. A spark of hope.

He hadn't used the morphine that day, or the next, or the next. By the time February rolled around, Michael's oncologist agreed to arrange a last-ditch round of immunotherapy.

And it had worked. Dear God, it had worked.

It was time to cash in on the old house. With his father's decline, it was ironic that his purchase of the place made it possible for Peter and his family to return to Maple City. To care for Big Bear in his waning days. It would be good for Michael too—get him out of the city and into the fresh air, even if it did occasionally smell like burnt pig.

"What stinks?" the boy yawned.

"That's the pork processing plant."

"Ewww."

"You'll get used to it, kiddo."

Hannah returned waving a key in her hand. She jumped into the car and glanced back at Peter. "What am I, your chauffeur?"

"What's a chauffeur?" Michael asked.

"Like an Uber driver but fancier," Peter said.

"We're around back. You want to follow me in the truck?"

Peter smiled and leaned back, arms over his head. "I'll get it later, Jeeves."

Michael mimicked his father, arms above his head as well. "Yeah, Jeeves."

Hannah shook her head. "Why I put up with you two is a mystery."

She pulled out of the parking lot and circled the motel, coming to a stop before their room.

"We've got a kitchenette," Hannah said proudly. "At no extra cost."

"That's my girl," Peter said.

While Michael checked out the TV channels, Peter and Hannah lay on the bed, shoes kicked to the corner.

It was no Manhattan apartment, but it would do for now. They were all together. And that was what was important.

"You ready for our new adventure, Mrs. Larson?"

"No. But when did that ever stop me?"

They kissed and snuggled close, content to watch as Michael flipped from channel to channel, surfing through his options.

* * *

The dark figure peered at the family from the shadows, hidden in the corner. Half of it longed to join them on the bed—the other half yearned to lash out, to strike.

To hurt.

The deadlock held it in place.

It would make itself known in time. But not yet. For now, the Messy Man was content to watch.

And wait...

AUTHOR'S NOTE

Last week, I told my wife that our house—and in particular the side that contains my office—was waking up. There was a time when we couldn't walk down the hallway without feeling the urge to glance over our shoulder or quicken our pace. But for the past few years, things have been relatively quiet.

That changed once I hit the home stretch of this book. I won't go through the laundry list of thumps and bumps and cold spots that cropped up—you'll just have to take my word when I say that writing this book has made this house once again…unquiet.

I'll leave you with the following unedited except from one of my last writing sessions. It seems that someone—or something—wasn't content to let me do all the typing:

> "As Peter crouched, helpless to stop the boy's progress,
> a notion struck him that was so simple and pure
> that000000000000000000000000000000000000000000000000
> 0000000000000"

I sincerely hope that my ethereal companion's addition of fifty-four zeroes was simply its desire to collaborate and not a message of a more nefarious nature. Time will tell.

Chris Sorensen
January 19, 2018

BIOGRAPHY

Chris Sorensen spends many days and nights locked away inside his own nightmare room. He is the narrator of over 200 audiobooks (including the award-winning *The Missing* series by Margaret Peterson Haddix) and the recipient of three AudioFile Earphone Awards. Over the past fifteen years, the Butte Theater and Thin Air Theatre Company in Cripple Creek, Colorado have produced dozens of his plays including *Dr. Jekyll's Medicine Show, Werewolves of Poverty Gulch* and *The Vampire of Cripple Creek.* He is the author of the middle grade book *The Mad Scientists of New* Jersey and has written numerous screenplays including *Suckerville, Bee Tornado* and *The Roswell Project.*

Coming soon...

THE HUNGRY ONES

THE MESSY MAN SERIES
BOOK 2

CHRIS SORENSEN

Harmful Monkey Press • Sparta, NJ

CPSIA information can be obtained
at www.ICGtesting.com
Printed in the USA
LVHW041243041118
595902LV00002B/401

ML NOV 2018